S. N. RAO

Mr. Niyogi's Last Audit

COPPER
PLATE

First published by Copperplate 2024

First edition

ISBN (print): 978-1-0689096-1-0
ISBN (digital): 978-1-0689096-0-3

Editing by Susan Gaigher
Cover art by Jonas Peres Studio

This book was professionally typeset on Reedsy.
Find out more at reedsy.com

For Babu

Acknowledgments

The book would not have been possible without the wholehearted encouragement that I received from my family and friends.

I also want to acknowledge all of those who have been part of my life and have contributed to shaping my experiences and imparted life lessons to me.

Chapter 1 - Mr. Niyogi

I was feeling cold, so I opened my eyes to find myself in a cold room. It was an unfamiliar room, and I could not recollect how I got here. The room was dimly lit. I did not know what time it was; the curtains were open, and it was dark outside. I needed to pee. I took a deep breath, turned onto my left side and pushed myself into a sitting position. My arms trembled with the effort, and I felt a pain in my left shoulder. The pain brought back some memories. I knew this room. I had been sleeping in this hotel room for a few days, but I wasn't sure for how long.

I pushed myself off the bed and started shuffling towards the bathroom. The grey socks I was wearing were making it harder to shuffle on the carpeted floor. Every muscle and bone in my body was aching.

The bathroom door was so heavy that I couldn't even push it with one hand. I had to put my shoulder to it while holding the door frame for support. The sight of the toilet was intensifying my urge to pee. I didn't know if I could hold it long enough to make it to the toilet. Again, I shuffled towards the toilet. I could barely hold it; I struggled to pull my pants down with my good hand and managed to sit down on the toilet just as a stream of pee pushed itself out. *Phew, that was close.*

I was already dreading getting up after I was done peeing. I heard someone knocking on the door of the room. "I am in the bathroom!" I tried to yell, but I doubted my voice reached beyond the bathroom door.

I heard the door opening. "Hellooo? Sir?" said the person that opened the door. It was a man's voice. I tried to hurry, pulling my pants up and shuffling to the bathroom door. I pulled open the heavy door and saw a man with a wheelchair. He was standing in the hallway of what appeared to be a hotel.

"Hello Mr. Niyogi," he said, "did you manage to get some sleep?"

"No, I did not," I said. "The pain was too much. Is it time to go already?"

"Yes sir," he said, not surprised by the question. "I was told to take you to the conference room at this time."

"Huh." *I hate this routine. I hate that I have to depend on all these people, all these strangers to take me places.* "What do you want me to do now?" I asked.

"Well sir," he said patiently, "let's get your sweater and sandals on, and let's go and get you some breakfast."

"I hate the food that you guys give me," I said. "I hate it that I have to take my food through this tube sticking out of my nose," I added, pointing to the small tube poking out of my left nostril.

"Nonetheless, you need the food sir," said the man. "You have a lot of work to do today. I was told that it is only for another week. So not for long."

Hearing that brought back some memories from the day before. The stacks of printed paper on a large oval table in a spacious conference room. The white walls and white chairs. "I would much rather be in my house with my wife than this hotel," I said, the irritation clear in my voice while I pulled myself towards the wheelchair that the man in the suit had placed near me.

It took a while to sit down in the wheelchair, but the guy waited patiently. Once seated, I asked him to bring me my glasses. With my glasses in hand, we set off to the conference room again. We descended five floors down to floor forty-three, where the conference room was. In the room I found my former colleague Kiran Singh already waiting for me, his computer open in front of him. Singh was very handy with computers and could do everything that I needed help with. I had lost the knowledge and patience to deal with computers a long time ago.

Seeing me, he came over and thanked the guy in the suit. Kiran then wheeled me to the other end of the table, where I had been sitting the day before. He handed me my green-ink ballpoint pen and headed back to his computer.

Seeing the huge stacks of documents in front of me, I felt so lost. "I don't know where to begin, Kiran. I don't know where I left off yesterday," I said to him.

"Mr. Niyogi, look at the yellow notepad on your right," he said cheerily. "It has information about what we are doing and where you left off last night."

To my right was a yellow notepad on which he had written the high-level objective of our task and some notes about where we left off the day before. I read the note once, twice, thrice, and by the fourth time, I started remembering the events of the previous day.

While I was reading the note, Kiran tapped on my shoulder and said, "Mr. Niyogi, let's get you some breakfast." He nodded to the back of the room, where I saw a floor-to-ceiling curtain. He wheeled me around the table and pushed my wheelchair towards the curtain. Behind the curtain was a young man standing next to a small table. On the table were two tall glasses containing a brown liquid, and next to the glasses was a largish syringe.

As my chair reached the table, the young man opened the stopper on the tube sticking out of my nose. He then sucked some of the liquid from the first glass into the syringe and attached the syringe to the tube. He lifted the syringe higher than the level of my nose and said, "Are you ready sir?"

I nodded, and he started squirting the liquid into the tube a little bit at a time. I felt the warm liquid in my feeding tube, but I didn't know what it tasted like. Slowly he emptied both the glasses, and I felt full, my belly warm on the inside.

I think there was coffee in the concoction because I started feeling my spirits lifting ever so slightly. After detaching the syringe and closing the stopper on the feeding tube, the young man gave me warm wet towel, and I dabbed my face with it. He then said to Kiran from across the room, "Mr. Niyogi's breakfast is done."

I heard Kiran's chair creaking, and then, after a few beats, I saw him pull back the curtain. He wheeled me back to the table with the stacks of documents. I had no interest in doing this work, but I had to do it; they needed me to do this audit. And so, my day of auditing began. I took the sheets of paper that I had been working on the night before, picked up my pen, put my glasses on and started at the top of the page.

I started reviewing the procedures that Saran Airlines followed when it came to their financial reporting practices. The audit that Kiran and I were performing was in preparation of an external audit that was to be performed by KPMG very soon. We had to finish the audit this week and then hand over the final reports to Mr. Saran.

Performing this audit had been hard so far. I had trouble reading, maintaining my focus and keeping my mind from wandering. It was extremely boring work; I found no joy in it. In fact, I found no joy in anything lately. Ever since this disease started ravaging my body and my ability to control my movements, joy had left me and moved on. It had been pain, despair and more pain since then.

Multiple times an hour, I had to remind myself of my reasons for doing this work just so I could keep going. I was making a lot of mistakes that Kiran was able to catch, thankfully. I only hoped that I would continue to be useful in doing this work and that Kiran's efforts in correcting my mistakes would not exceed my worth.

Before this audit started, I had helped Kiran with identifying some fraudulent transactions that had helped the airline to recover a lot of money—or at least trace the lost money. I had been able to do that by working with Kiran a few hours every week, but this task required a much more significant time commitment.

I did not need to do this work while I struggled with my ailment, but I had to do it. I was hoping that it would give me bargaining power to get Mr. Saran to agree to what I was going to ask him once I finished the audit. Saran Airlines already had to accommodate my numerous needs by providing a full-time nurse, a therapist and all the equipment that I needed to stay in this hotel so I could do this work. I would have to give him enough value to make up for all the extra money they had to spend to allow me to work and to make what I was going to ask him seem like reasonable compensation.

"Kiran, can you come here one second?" I said to Kiran. I had noticed something. "I am looking at the list of people that are to be involved in the payment-release process. I see that it is possible for one person from the accounts payable department to receive an invoice from a vendor, enter it into the system and even approve the payment after uploading the invoice. We should separate those duties. We should have a junior associate enter the invoices received, but have a senior team member review the same before payment can be approved."

"Understood sir. What about releasing the payment?"

"That is a good point. It would be good to limit that to a manager who can actually release the payments. And we should standardize all payments so that only direct deposits to the vendor's bank account are allowed. No payments by cheque or cash."

"Well sir, as you know, we work with a lot of small vendors, many of whom are located in rural areas with no easy access to bank accounts. Direct deposits may not always work."

"Yes, agreed. In that case, we should have a cap on the cash payments that can be released. Anything above ₹10,000 should only be paid out via bank transfer to a single vendor. Or even better, send them the money via UPI to their mobile wallets."

"Noted, sir. I will update that in the procedural recommendations document and share it with the CFO for review."

Kiran went back to his computer, and I resumed going through the document in front of me.

Saran Airlines had started out as a bus transport company and slowly grew into offering passenger transit via small aircrafts and small boats and ferries. Before I retired from working with the company, I was head of their finance department. After I retired from work, I took care of my wife Ramani for many years.

The last few years, Parkinson's disease started creeping up on me, and slowly but surely, even the most basic things like walking became difficult. I used to spend hours reading the *Deccan Herald*, my favourite newspaper, but soon, reading and then writing also became difficult. And slowly I went from taking care of Ramani to being taken care of by Ramani, my daughter Archana and even a full-time nurse.

Then the COVID-19 pandemic arrived and locked us all down in the house, bringing an end to the little bit of walking I used to do.

I tried to put aside all that troubled me to help Saran Airlines with this audit. While I was in the conference room doing this work, I would sometimes stop to take a look out at the horizon. The view from the forty-third floor showed me the whole northeast side of Bengaluru. This building did not exist when I was working for Saran Airlines before my retirement. As Bengaluru expanded and the need for office space grew in the city, many older factories that had stopped being profitable became the locations for tall office buildings and hotels.

The building I was in housed a hotel spread across twenty floors, private residences that occupied another twenty floors and offices that took up the remaining thirty floors. Saran Airlines had its offices in this building in addition to the main office in the heart of old Bengaluru.

I felt a tap on my shoulder, and my focus snapped back to the work I was supposed to be doing. I looked to my left and saw Kiran standing there with a sheet of paper.

"Sir, I have a question about this process of filing the documentation that we expect from the vendors..." Kiran continued with his question, and I tried my best to answer him. We continued working for two more hours before I said that I wanted to take a bathroom break and that I then needed to lie down. The conference room had an attached bathroom. The nurse who had helped feed me earlier came to my side when he heard what I needed. He unlocked the wheels of my chair and took me to the bathroom.

After I was done in the bathroom, he then wheeled me to a couch behind the curtain that was on one side of the room. With help from the nurse, I lay down on the couch and tried to stretch my legs. My need to take regular breaks to lie down was surely slowing us down, but Kiran and Mr. Saran tolerated it.

Since I knew how the company operated when it was much smaller than it was now, I understood the historical context as to why certain decisions were taken. Thus, what I brought to the table was helping Kiran and Saran Airlines understand why the company operated the way it did and what needed to be done before it would clear the external audits required to become a publicly traded company.

I was about to drift off to sleep on the couch when an alarm went off on the nurse's phone. He looked at it and started pounding some tablets into powder before mixing them into a glass of water.

"Time for your medicine, Mr. Niyogi," he said. He took out a syringe from his bag, sucked the water into it and injected the same into my feeding tube. I had to take the medicine four times a day, as it helped to keep my Parkinson's symptoms in check. My doctors had told me that it was all I could do. I had to keep taking the medicine to control the symptoms of this disease, but there was no cure.

I had started with taking the medication once a day, then it became twice and eventually increased to four times a day. The medicine was horrible and caused all kinds of side effects, but if I stopped taking it, I would not be able to function at all; if what I had become could even be called functioning.

There was nothing I could do about it, and I had spent many months worrying about it already. Now all that I wanted to do was focus on this work and try to finish it in the next seven days so I could ask for what I wanted from Mr. Saran.

Chapter 2 - Kiran Singh

Mr. Niyogi was struggling to even hold the pen well enough to write his notes and remarks on the sheets of paper in front of him. His Parkinson's disease had taken a major toll on him. He was always such a nice person to work with. Always had such a pleasant demeanour; always kind. He never used to reprimand anyone for the mistakes they made at work. He would immediately get us all to start working on fixing the mistakes. It was so nice to work for him.

And as happy as I was to be working with him again, I couldn't think of any reason why he would want to do what he was doing. Away from his family, without their knowledge, here he was, back to being an accountant, back to doing what he had done for more than forty years of his healthy adult life.

I saw him staring out the floor-to-ceiling windows at the view of the northeast side of the city. The pen was hanging loosely in his hands. His back was hunched, and his shoulders were drooping. It looked like he was slowly sinking into his chair.

"Are you doing okay Mr. Niyogi?" I asked him, startling him.

"Uhhhh?...I am okay, I just feel tired," he whispered, looking down at the documents on the table, but not really seeing them.

I remembered that I was supposed to call in the physiotherapist whenever I saw that happening. I picked up my phone and sent a message to Nurse Mary.

'Hi Mary, Mr. Niyogi has paused his work and is staring into the distance. I was asked to let you know if that happens,' I wrote in my message.

'Okay, coming,' was the reply I got from her.

Five minutes later, there was a polite knock on the door and in walked Nurse Mary. She was around thirty-five years old, short and slim. She walked with purpose, back straight and taking long strides. She was pulling a stationary bike on a base with wheels behind her. The whole machine looked heavy, but she had no trouble pulling it.

"Hello Mr. Niyogi," said Mary with her usual loud and firm voice, "how are you doing today? Did you have your breakfast?"

Mr. Niyogi looked at Mary and nodded. He did not say a word, but knowing what was going to happen next, he put his pen down and pushed his wheelchair away from the table. Then he started to get up from the chair slowly and painfully.

"It is time for your workout Mr. Niyogi," said Mary, locking the castors of the base and plugging the stationary bike into a nearby power outlet. Mary then guided Mr. Niyogi to the seat on the bike and gently placed his feet on the pedals. She then secured his feet to the pedals with straps. Mr. Niyogi held on to the handlebars, and Mary pressed a few buttons. The pedals started moving. Even though Mr. Niyogi was not making the pedals move, the movement still caused him pain. He was straining with the effort, but Mary pretended not to see the pain that was apparent in his face. She put a gentle hand on his back to encourage him, but that gentle hand had the effect of making Mr. Niyogi exert more effort to make the pedals go faster.

This went on for thirty minutes. By the end, Mr. Niyogi was sweating; he was spent. When Mary pressed a few more buttons, the pedals slowly came to a stop. Mr. Niyogi also stopped pedalling, and a look of relief spread across his face. He got off the bike as quickly as he could, and there was a sense of urgency to his shuffles as he went back to the wheelchair he had been sitting in earlier.

"Mr. Niyogi," said Mary in her usual cheery voice, "biking will help release dopamine in your body, and it will make you feel better. You should try and do this for longer than thirty minutes next time, or try pedalling faster."

"Yes Mary...I will...next time," said Mr. Niyogi. I think he was hoping his assurance would satisfy Mary and that she would go away. This was the first of such workouts today, and he usually had to go through this a few more times on a typical day to be able to get through the work he was doing. Today was the tenth day of the audit. And there was still a long way to go.

Mr. Niyogi sat up a little straighter, picked up his pen and put on his glasses. He looked to have found the focus to get back to his work. He started reading the documents in front of him, occasionally making notes in the margin. We continued to work for two more hours without a break before he needed to use the washroom. The nurse took him to the washroom, then gave him his medication and a cup of coffee through his feeding tube so he could get back to work.

After lunch and more bathroom breaks, we were close to the end of the workday, and I could see that Mr. Niyogi was hanging on by a thread. He was tired and was having a hard time getting his hand to write. At last, he couldn't take it anymore and said, "Kiran, can you call Mary and ask for an impulse-therapy session?"

"Are you sure sir? If you are tired, we can continue tomorrow. I hate to see you taking so much pains for this work. I am sure all of this is not more important than conserving your health."

"What will I achieve by conserving my health, Kiran? At least this way I am of some use to someone."

"Don't say that sir, you have worked hard all your life for so many organizations, for your family, and you have served so many people through your work with the lion's club. You deserve to rest now, sir."

"I could rest, but the rest is not going to bring anything back. It is not going to make me younger or even healthier again. Just let me do this work; there is nothing else I want more right now. "

I sighed. There was nothing I could say to convince him to take it easy. He was bent upon punishing himself and continuing this strenuous work.

I messaged Mary again and asked her to come administer an impulse-therapy session. Mary responded that she would be there soon. Mary was from the same physiotherapy center that Mr. Niyogi had been going to for the last few weeks. She had been engaged to be available full time to administer therapy whenever Mr. Niyogi needed it.

A few minutes later, another gentle knock on the door was followed by Mary opening the door and using the door stopper to keep it open. She then pulled a gurney into the room. It was unlike any normal gurney I had ever seen. It had a multitude of wires connected to a box mounted underneath it, and there was also a control panel with a display near the head of the gurney.

Mary moved the gurney close to the floor-to-ceiling windows and plugged it into a wall outlet nearby. She then came over to Mr. Niyogi's wheelchair and moved it to the gurney.

"Can you get on the bed, Mr. Niyogi?" she asked, taking his extended hand to support him as he struggled to stand up. Again, she displayed a strength that I would not have attributed to her size in helping Mr. Niyogi stand. Mr. Niyogi was five feet ten inches tall, and Mary was only five foot two.

Mr. Niyogi slowly got onto the gurney and lay down. Mary helped lift his legs onto the gurney and pulled a thin sheet over him up to his waist.

She then proceeded to turn him onto his side and while holding him with one hand, connected a few probes to his spine. She slowly turned him onto his back and adjusted the sheet before going to the control panel and pressing a few keys.

A low hum emanated from the machines on the gurney, with occasional beeps. Sometimes Mr. Niyogi would flinch when it beeped, but other times he stayed calm and stared at the ceiling. This continued for the twenty minutes that the therapy lasted.

I walked over to where Mary was standing behind the control panel and asked her, "What exactly is this therapy for?"

"Well, I have connected small electrodes to a few places on Mr. Niyogi's spine. The beeps that you hear, those are when a small electrical impulse is sent to the spot the electrode is attached to. What this does is it sends these electrical signals to Mr. Niyogi's brain, and it acts like a stimulant. This stimulation temporarily improves Mr. Niyogi's ability to control his movements. It also suppresses a common symptom of Parkinson's, which is the uncontrolled muscle spasms experienced by people suffering from it.

"I don't exactly know all the scientific reasons behind why this works, but it does work, and we have been offering this therapy at our clinic for a few years now. It has helped many patients get temporary relief from these symptoms."

I wanted to ask if there was really no cure for Parkinson's, as I had heard people say that often, but I did not want to ask it with Mr. Niyogi so close and able to hear what we were talking about.

"Thanks Mary," I said and walked back to my computer.

Once the twenty minutes were up, Mary once again turned Mr. Niyogi onto one side and detached the probes. She wiped his spine with a clean cloth before pulling down his shirt and turning him back onto his back.

"Do you want to lie down here for a while sir, or do you want to get up?" she asked.

Mr. Niyogi was already halfway to sitting up. He continued and sat up fully. He stretched his arms out, and he looked like he was ready to jump off the bed and take off. This therapy did really seem to give him an energy boost and control over his movements that I had not seen the whole day.

Mary then assisted Mr. Niyogi off the bed, and instead of sitting down in his wheelchair, he got behind it and used the chair to support him as he took a few steps towards the bathroom. He paused to check if he was okay to continue and then walked to the bathroom a little faster than his usual shuffle. The male nurse who had been sitting down quickly got behind him to help him in the bathroom.

Mr. Niyogi came out of the bathroom looking a little fresher. He must have splashed his face with water while in there. He asked for something to drink and then proceeded to his spot at the table. Then he put on his glasses and picked up his pen before starting to read the documents in front of him.

He was able to continue working like this for another hour and then decided to end the day.

"I want to go and lie down now Kiran," he said, pushing his chair away from the table, "let's continue tomorrow."

"Yes sir," I said, "let's continue tomorrow."

The nurse came up to his wheelchair and started to wheel him to the door. I quickly packed my bags, locked up the conference room, and caught up with Mr. Niyogi as he was nearing the elevator.

I got into the elevator and decided to go with Mr. Niyogi to his room. When we reached his room, I opened the door with the key that the nurse handed me. I held the door open, and I followed Mr. Niyogi and the nurse into the room.

Mr. Niyogi wanted to sit on the sofa next to his bed, and once the wheelchair reached the sofa, he got up and moved to sit on it. There was always a noticeable difference in Mr. Niyogi's movements before and after a therapy session. The improvement usually lasted a few hours after the biking session and significantly longer after the impulse therapy.

I sat down in the chair that was beside the sofa and waited for the nurse to go out. The nurse would usually take a break for an hour or so every day after our work ended.

"Sir, can I ask you a question?" I asked Mr. Niyogi after the nurse left. "Why don't you want your family to know that you are doing this work?"

"I must have told this to you before Kiran, but I feel like I have become such a big burden to them that I don't want to add this to their worries too. Right now, they think I am in the hospital in isolation. I call home every day to ensure that they know that I am getting plenty of rest in the 'hospital' and that they should not worry."

"I don't know if I fully agree with your reasons sir, but I respect your wishes. Anyway, I will head home now sir, and I will see you tomorrow."

After leaving the room, I gently closed the door behind me and headed home, just hoping that I was not contributing in any way to worsen Mr. Niyogi's health. I also hoped that his family wouldn't end up coming to the conclusion that somehow, I was the one that coerced or convinced him to take on this project. None of those things were in my control, and my loyalties rested with Mr. Niyogi. I wanted to do all that I could to help him do what he wished to do.

The following day, I reached the conference room before Mr. Niyogi got there, and I saw that Mr. Niyogi's nurse had already taken care of resupplying the room with everything Mr. Niyogi would need throughout the day.

About ten minutes later, I heard a knock on the door, and I quickly walked over to open it. Mr. Niyogi was sitting in his wheelchair, dressed in a chequered shirt, grey sweatpants, white socks and white canvas shoes. He looked tired and had what looked like a two-week-old beard. When I used to work with him before he retired, his hair was much blacker, and he never went without a shave. He lifted his right palm towards me and said, "Hi, Kiran."

I had not heard a good morning or good evening from Mr. Niyogi's mouth in a while. I believed it was because for him, it was never a good morning, evening or night. He was probably just surviving what his ailment had inflicted on his mind and body.

Seeing him like this once again evoked a pang of guilt within my mind for what I was doing to add to his suffering. I had to put those feelings aside and continue the work we had started. Maybe by finishing this work as soon as possible, we could relieve Mr. Niyogi from the obligation he felt that made him want to do this work in the first place.

I held the door open to let Mr. Niyogi in. "Good morning, Mr. Niyogi," I said. "Good morning, buddy," I said to the nurse as I closed the door once they were inside.

"Did you get some rest last night sir?"

"Yes Kiran, I did as much as I could," said Mr. Niyogi.

His wheelchair was in his usual spot, stopped there by the nurse. My Niyogi fished his glasses out from his pocket and put them on. Then he searched for his pen, which he found under a few sheets of paper.

"What are we looking at today?" he asked.

"Well, sir, today we will be looking at the reporting and bookkeeping processes followed by the maintenance and engineering departments. We want to understand their processes and recommend changes to bring them onto the same standard that we are recommending for the rest of the departments that we reviewed."

"Are we looking at all types of maintenance? Don't the maintenance departments of various types of transportation operate separately at this moment?"

"Yes sir, road, airlines and water transport maintenance departments are all separate at this moment. And they are managed by separate department heads. The aircraft maintenance team is the one that is most streamlined at this moment because they were already a well-oiled operation when we acquired them. It is the road and water transport departments that have the most disparities, as each city's maintenance shop is run with its own best practices as dictated by the local chief mechanic. "

"I see," said Mr. Niyogi, pausing for a few seconds before adding, "they may not like it, but we should find out which of the maintenance shops are the most efficient and see if we can implement those same policies and practices across the organization."

"What do you need to assess their current practices, sir? I already asked all the city maintenance departments to share the reporting practices they follow, and I also have the account statements from the last two years."

"I will start with their account statements and their books. Usually looking at the books can reveal a lot about which departments know what they are doing and which are managed poorly."

The rest of the day, Mr. Niyogi and I continued to work on the audit as we raced to finish the work sooner rather than later.

Chapter 3 - Mr. Niyogi

Everything hurts. My hands, my knees, ankles, my back. Everything. Why must it hurt so much? When will the pain stop? I must get up now, but I don't feel like getting out of bed.

It has been so many days since I saw my wife and daughter. I wonder how they are doing without me. I should have just stayed with them.

Aah, who am I kidding? Haven't I put them through enough? The last few years until I came here, they have not had a single night of peaceful sleep. No time for themselves. All they have done is take care of me. Day in and day out. And most recently, when I could not even bathe myself or even get up by myself to go to the bathroom, they had to help me take a piss or poop right next to the bed and clean up after me. Maybe they are better off without me.

Since I got this disease, I can't even walk well by myself. If I try to walk, I fall down. My feet lock up and I can't move. I start to lean forward, but my feet don't move, and I start to fall...but I cannot afford to fall. I cannot afford to stop working now. Two hundred people are depending on me to complete this audit. I have to rescue them.

They need me more than anything.

* * *

Three Months Earlier

It was around six in the evening, and I was in bed looking at the bit of sky that was visible from the window of my bedroom. It was December of 2021. For the bigger part of the year, my wife and I had been locked up in the apartment. My daughter was locked up in hers. The COVID restrictions had immobilized us, but in the last few months, things were slowly opening up again.

My daughter, who had been working from home for more than a year, had started going to her office again recently. She usually returned home around five in the evening. After freshening up, she would come to our apartment, which was in the same apartment complex but on a different floor.

I heard my daughter walking into the apartment and talking to Ramani. She then came into my room and asked me how I was feeling when her phone rang.

"Dad, someone's calling, I will talk to them and come back, okay?"

I nodded and turned to gaze out of the window again.

"Hi Gopika, how are you?" my daughter said to the person on the phone. "It has been so long ya, what is happening in your life?" My daughter was on the call for a while, and I listened to her side of the conversation.

"Uh uh."

"Oh my God!"

"Really?"

"That must have been so hard ya, how did you manage?"

"All alone?"

At long last she cut the call and turned to me. "That was Gopika, my classmate from college," she said. "Gopika said that she has been struggling to get her son Rajamouli back home. Her son went to work for this mining company after completing his chemical engineering degree, and he had to travel to a mining island called Khiyalee in the

Maldives. The island is owned by the mining company. He has been there for the past two years, and a few months back, the company sadly went bankrupt, leaving all the people who were on the island with no means of travelling back to their homes."

"Why?" I managed to whisper. Even talking was hard. It seemed like my voice was deteriorating faster than the rest of my body, if that was even possible.

"The island is very remote and far from the main islands of the Maldives. And the only way to the island is by boat," said Archana. "Because the mining company has gone bankrupt, it does not have any money to send a rescue boat. The company owners are in the wind; no one can find them. The island is so remote that the people who are stuck there have no way of leaving. It is so sad."

"How many people are on the island?"

"Around two hundred people, it seems. Oh well, what we can do? Maybe the government will do something."

Archana's phone rang again, and she left the room to talk. I drifted into sleep and only woke up when I had to pee again.

"Manoj!" I called out to the full-time caretaker my daughter had hired to take care of everything I needed. "Manoj!" I called out again, this time a bit louder.

"Yes sir, coming!" I heard Manoj say, and a few moments later he was by my bedside.

"I need to pee," I said. Manoj went into the bathroom and got the urine bottle for me to pee in. After I was done, he took it back into the washroom to throw away the pee.

I drifted back into sleep.

"Niyogi!" I heard someone calling me. "Mr. Niyogi, can you help us? Can you help us get home? Please help us...if you can hear me, you are our only hope."

I looked around to see who was speaking but saw no one. I could hear the TV in the living room; maybe the voice was coming from the TV.

"Mr. Niyogi, I know you can hear me, please help us."

"I can't help you; how can I help you?" I said to the voice, "I can barely stand, let alone help you in any way. I can't help you."

"Please...Mr. Niyogi, please do something and help us, only you can," the voice said.

"How can I help? I am bedridden, and I can't help myself in any way. How can I help you?"

"Please sir, help us," the voice pleaded, "we need a boat to come back home; a large boat. That is all we are asking for, nothing more. Just a large boat so we can get home, so I can get home to my mother."

"I don't know who you are, and I don't have a boat that I can send to you."

"You know who I am, Mr. Niyogi. Your daughter just told you about me. She told you how my mother was struggling to get people to help her."

"Are you Gopika's son? Rajamouli?" I asked in the darkness.

"I am Rajamouli, and I am here with so many of my colleagues. There is no one to hear our pleas for help. Only you can help us Mr. Niyogi, I know you can."

"I cannot! That is so silly, how can I help? I have nothing."

"Please don't say that you cannot help us sir, we have no one else that we can ask. You are the only one who can hear me..."

"I can't, I can't, I CANNOT!!!" I yelled back.

"Mr. Niyogi?"

"Dad?"

I saw Manoj and my daughter standing in front of me. "Do you need something?" my daughter asked.

"Huh? What?" I said, not fully understanding what had happened.

"You were saying that you cannot. What do you need?"

"Nothing, nothing. Must have been a dream."

"Oh, okay," said my daughter, starting to leave the room. "I will come see you later, Dad," she added, walking away. Manoj stayed for a couple more seconds, then he too left the room.

"Mr. Niyogi," I heard a voice whisper, "you have to help us. Please do something."

"I can't," I whispered back. "I am sick and confined to this bed. I can't."

* * *

My days were always the same; they started in bed and ended in bed—except for getting up to be fed through the tube in my nose and to take a shower. It was always the same. How long could I go on like this? When would this end?

"Mr. Niyogi," the voice interrupted my thoughts, "please help us."

Am I going crazy? What is going on? Am I hallucinating?

"Mr. Niyogi..." the whisper faded away.

I did not hear anything for a few hours. But I couldn't put the thought of those people out of my head. What were those people going through, stuck on the mining island?

Do they have enough food? Do they have enough medical supplies to help the injured if there are any injuries to take care of? Do they have electricity to keep themselves comfortable in the heat? Do they have phone and internet connections to communicate with their families? Maybe next time the boy speaks to me I can ask him about these. Am I going crazy? Is the voice just in my head? So silly of me to think that I am actually talking to that boy.

"Mr. Niyogi, can you please do something to help us? I know that you are a kind person, sir. I know that you are a go-getter. I believe that you can do anything. Only you can help us, please," the voice said when it returned.

"Do you have enough food to survive on?" I asked. I remembered that I should not be talking too loudly, otherwise my family might think that I was going crazy, and they would get unnecessarily worried. I put my elbow over my face so that people couldn't see my mouth from the door if anyone walked in suddenly. "Do you have enough food?" I whispered this time.

"That is not important Mr. Niyogi," said the voice, sounding annoyed, "what is important is that I want to go back home, and that is all that I want you to worry about."

"What do you mean food is not important? How about medical supplies; do you have enough medical supplies?"

"Why are you asking me these irrelevant questions Mr. Niyogi? I cannot answer these questions. I just want to go home. Why do you want to know if there is food here?"

"I want to know so I can understand how much time you have; I am sure sooner or later someone will come to help you, and I want to know if you have enough food to survive on until they come to help you."

"We have some food, but it won't last long. We are two hundred people on this island. We had some paddle boats, and some of us already took those boats and tried to go home, but the sea was too rough, so they turned back. There are not enough boats for us all."

Ramani walked into the room. "Do you want anything dear?" she asked, "I heard you saying something. Do you want water?"

"No, no. I'm not saying anything," I said. "I don't want anything. Did you eat?" Ramani was always thinking of me. I very rarely saw her eat anything, since I hardly left the room.

"I ate a while back. Are you hungry? Do you want something to eat?"

Ever since the muscles in my throat became weak, I had not been able to eat anything by myself. I could chew, but I couldn't swallow. The only way for me to consume food was through a feeding tube that went into my stomach through my nose.

Even though we both knew that I couldn't eat anything by myself, Ramani was careful not to remind me of that. Whenever she asked me about food, she would ask as if I could eat by myself. The same weakness of my throat muscles made it difficult for me to talk; my vocal cords had also become too weak.

"No, I am not hungry."

"Okay, call me if you need anything," said Ramani before walking out of the room.

After Ramani left, I realized that I didn't hear any strange voices when someone else was in the room with me. I must have been imagining the voice. No one had been talking to me. I didn't want to tell Ramani that I was hearing voices; she already has enough reasons to worry about me.

What are all the different ways that the boy stuck on the island can be brought back home? What if someone writes to the Maldivian government? Did Gopika contact the Indian government? Who do I know who can help? I don't know anyone who has a boat. Let alone a boat that can carry two hundred people. Can any private company help? I am sure there are a lot of boats sitting idle because of all the travel restrictions all over the world. Maybe some shipping company can send an unused boat to pick up the people from the island.

I remember Saran Airlines had a flight to the Maldives, and they used to pick up passengers from the various nearby islands to bring them to the airport free of charge. Maybe Saran Airlines can send one of their boats in the Maldives to this island and pick up the people to bring them home. I am sure Saran Airlines is rich enough that they can spare one big boat.

I used to work for Saran Airlines a long time ago, back when I was well and did not have this disease. I used to be their lead accountant. The chairman of the airline was a nice guy. He used to take good care of all his employees. I wonder if they still fly to the Maldives.

Well, even if they are, what can I do about it? I can't go to talk to Saran

Airlines; I can barely talk. I don't know if they would even recognize me if I call on them.

It is sad, but I can't do anything to help these people. I am sure the government will do something to bring them back. The Indian Navy has many ships that must operate in that area, or perhaps the Indian Coast Guard can send someone.

I am sure India is sending medical supplies and provisions to the Maldives to help the country cope with the pandemic. Maybe on the way back, one of the supply ships can stop on the island and pick up these people.

For a country like India, two hundred people is nothing, and Indian Navy ships can handle much bigger rescues, I am sure.

I don't know why these people think that I can help them. Maybe when I was younger and active in the Lion's Club, I could have at least petitioned the government to take action; but not now. I have barely spoken to anyone other than my wife and daughter in the last year. I have not stepped out of the house in so many months, let alone been able to take a step by myself without any help.

I can't even control my bladder very well; I had to start wearing adult diapers. It was beyond embarrassing, but I could not do anything about it. I could not keep peeing in my bed and expecting Ramani or my daughter or Manoj to keep changing the sheets.

Even if I manage to talk to someone and ask them to help, this is not a simple matter. This is not like booking a taxi to take someone from one end of the city to another. These people are on an island hundreds if not thousands of kilometers away from Indian shores. It would cost a fortune to hire a boat and bring them back to India. And it would be hell navigating the bureaucracy to get the required permission from not only the Indian government but also from the government of the Maldives. That is no easy task.

And so another few days passed, or maybe it was a week—I did not know. All I could think of was my painful existence. I didn't know when

I would be relieved from all this pain and suffering. I couldn't bear it.

Chapter 4 - Archana

Ever since I spoke to my dad about my friend's son being stuck on the mining island, he has been staying awake more. Before, he used to spend most of the day napping or sleeping. At night, his sleep was usually interrupted many times due to him waking up with body pains. He used to also sleep a lot during the day, but now he was staying awake during the day too, thinking about something.

I wondered if I had made a mistake by telling him about Gopika's son; he had his own health to worry about. Whenever I passed by his room door, he would be mumbling something to himself. Looking around as if someone was calling him. Whenever I asked him about it, he would dismiss it as nothing. But I suspected that he was sitting there in his room worrying about Gopika's son. It had always been like that, even before he got sick. If he heard that someone was having some problem, he would keep thinking about them and he would keep trying to come up with ideas on how to help them.

He would then go up to them and tell them how they could solve their problem. And until their problem was solved or it went away, he would always try and follow up to find out if the problem still persisted.

Since he heard about the boy being stuck on the island, he has been trying to get up and sit up more often than usual. Every time he tried to get up, he would wince with pain. I thought that he was very troubled knowing that the boy was unable to go home. He has become very restless.

I decided to go see him after work and ask him if he was worried about anything.

* * *

"Hi Dad," I called out to him when I went to his room. Manoj was changing his shirt. "How are you?"

He gave me a feeble smile that did a poor job of hiding his pain.

"Did you eat already? Do you want coffee?" I asked him. He shook his head, but he gestured for me to come and sit next to him.

"Gopika...son..." he managed to say, using his hands to gesture a question.

"Oh him, poor boy, no change in their situation," I said, having spoken to Gopika a couple of days earlier. "They are still on the island. They have no connectivity, so we don't know what is happening or how they are managing their food, etc."

My dad nodded. His brows came together, and it seemed that this news was causing him to worry. I wanted to ease the pressure on him and said, "I am sure someone will do something soon, Dad. Don't worry. There is nothing that we can do anyway." He nodded again.

"Government?" he asked. I assumed he was asking if the government was doing something about it.

"Apparently, the current government is in chaos, and there is a possible regime change happening there. And so, the government is in no position to do something about this. There is no one in the government to even listen. Plus, it is a private island; there is not much the government can or will do," I said, remembering what Gopika had told me earlier. "But it's okay; something will happen soon. I am sure there is a way to resolve this problem."

He sat there not saying anything for a while. Then he turned to me and asked, "Navy? Army? Indian?"

"I am sure it is not easy to get help from the Navy or Army unless the matter goes to the top levels of the Indian government. At a time when the Maldivian government is in such a delicate state, any action taken by Indian armed forces could send the wrong signal, and it may lead to an international incident. I don't think it is going to be that easy."

"What else has...Gopika tried?"

"Well, she has tried to reach out to the Indian Red Cross Society, but they are busy fighting the pandemic. They have no resources to spare for anything else."

"Hmm; so sad. What will she do?"

"I don't know Dad, but it is very sad indeed."

My dad became quiet for a while. I went out of the room, saying that I would be back soon. I spent some time helping my mom in the kitchen and went back to Dad's room after a bit. He was waiting for me, still sitting up. I went and sat down next to him.

"Do you know...what is Kiran Singh...doing nowadays?" Dad asked, really struggling to get the words out.

I knew Kiran Singh was Dad's old colleague from his Saran Airlines days, but I had no idea where he was now.

"I don't know Dad," I said, "but I will look online to see if I can find out. Why do you ask?"

"No reason..." said my dad, "I don't...why I remembered..."

I made a mental note to check for Kiran Singh online when I got to my computer. I checked the time and realized that I had to get back home; my son would be back soon, and he did not have his own keys.

I told my dad that I needed to go, and I left.

Later in the day, I searched online for Kiran Singh. It turned out that

Kiran was still working for Saran Airlines. He was still in the accounting department. I checked to see if I could get his number. I reached out to him on social media asking if he could share his number.

Sometime later, Kiran Singh messaged back with his phone number. I asked him for a good time to talk, and the next day I called him.

"Mr. Singh, how are you?" I asked him after he picked up the call. "I am Archana, Mr. Niyogi's daughter. Is this a good time to talk to you?"

"Yes, madam, of course," he said, "how is Mr. Niyogi doing? It has been such a long time since I spoke to him. I did not see him and did not get a chance to talk to him after he left Saran Airlines."

"He is...doing okay," I said. "To tell you the truth, he is suffering from Parkinson's disease, and it has taken a toll on him. He is mostly limited to his bed. Even his food consumption is through a feeding tube."

"Oh no," Mr. Singh said, "I never knew that our beloved Mr. Niyogi was so unwell. Very sorry to hear that. It must be very difficult for you all at home. How are you all coping with this? How is Mrs. Niyogi doing?"

"She is somehow managing with all of this, doing the best she can," I said.

"I understand how hard Parkinson's can be on the person suffering and the family members taking care of such a person. I have a close relative who also had Parkinson's. I feel so sad for how things have turned out," said Mr. Singh. "Is there anything that I can do to help? Was there anything in particular that you wanted to talk to me about?"

"Actually," I said, taking a deep breath, "my dad was remembering you the other day, and I was hoping to ask you to come and see him. I feel that it will do him good to see his friends. And my father always speaks very fondly of you. I completely understand if you cannot come, but I wanted to ask you nonetheless."

"Oh of course, I would love to come and see Mr. Niyogi," said Kiran, "I was going to ask you if I could come to see him. Please send me your address and also let me know when I can come."

"Thank you," I said, "that would be great. I just wanted to warn you that my dad has suffered a lot because of his ailment, and you may be surprised by how different he looks now. Please do not be shocked, or at least try not to show how shocked you are when you see him."

"Of course, of course," he said, "I will do my best."

I sent him my parents' home address and also asked if he could come the following weekend. He said that he would.

That evening, I told my dad about my conversation with Kiran Singh, and he nodded with a smile. He seemed to look forward to seeing Kiran. He usually always avoided people, but this time he seemed to look forward to the visit.

The weekend rolled around, and at around 4 p.m. on a Saturday, Mr. Kiran Singh knocked on my parents' door. I opened the door, and he stepped in with a small basket of fruit.

I took the basket from him, thanking him.

"How are you, Mr. Singh? Please take a seat," I said to him, "I will bring my dad here."

Dad had asked us to help him get into pants. He usually wore a simple cotton shirt with cotton shorts at home, but for this meeting with Kiran, he wanted to look better dressed.

With me on one side and my mom on the other, we walked my dad from the bedroom to the living room. My dad's eyes were focused on the floor ahead, willing his feet to keep moving. The colour drained from Mr. Singh's face as he watched in disbelief how frail my dad looked and how hard it was for him to walk. He regained his composure just in time before my dad looked up at him.

By the time my dad reached the sofa where Kiran was sitting, Kiran was smiling broadly. He started talking to dad as if they were back in the office of Saran Airlines together. He seemed to be doing his best to not show how he was feeling on the inside. He was jovial and was telling Dad what was happening at the office and how things changed after he left.

I could see that my dad was doing his best to make his conversation seem as effortless as possible. It was not entirely working, but he seemed to be trying.

"How has COVID affected the company?" my dad asked Kiran.

"Same as the whole transport industry sir," said Kiran, "we were practically grounded. It has been very tough. Thankfully Mr. Saran was able to get some government contracts to transport people and vaccinations to various parts of the country, and that has kept us afloat. It is not good money, profits are down, but it has kept us from incurring a loss. And we all kept our jobs. "

Kiran stayed for a whole hour, telling my dad all about the office, what new projects were going on, who left, who was still with the company and so on. He also told my dad about some slip-ups in accounting that led to some money going missing. It ended up costing the company close to ₹20 million, and they were still trying to trace the lost revenue.

"In all the years that you were working at Saran Airlines, sir, we never had any cases where money was unaccounted for at any of the branches. You kept everything running very efficiently, sir, and I unfortunately did not get to learn all of your methods from you before you retired," said Kiran.

My dad nodded with a smile.

Kiran then turned towards me and Mom and said, "If Mr. Niyogi was still working at Saran Airlines, I am sure he would have been able to track down the lost money without any problems. He was that good; I mean, he is that good when it comes to investigating money matters."

"Really Dad? You never told us that you were a money detective," I said and laughed.

"Mr. Niyogi was an expert in this domain, specifically with tracing where every rupee went by applying the methods of forensic account- ing," said Kiran. "We had so many people trying to rob the company, and he was always a few steps ahead of the scammers and fraudsters. He never allowed any entry to be made without complete traceability. We still follow the guidelines that was set by him in our Bengaluru branch, but we don't have much control over other offices. Especially since we acquired a few companies recently, and all of them follow their own accounting practices."

Hearing that his work was still considered to have been of a high standard brought a smile to my dad's face. He was beaming while Kiran spoke about the impact of his years at Saran. But the more he heard about it, the smile slowly faded away and he became serious, and at long last, I could see a tear rolling down from one of his eyes.

Kiran Singh also seemed to realize the impact his words were having on my dad. He quickly told him not to worry about it and to focus on getting better. He then said his goodbyes, gave my dad a hug and soon left.

"It was nice..." said my dad after he left, "to see Kiran after all this time."

After Kiran left and we helped Dad get back to his room, I asked him, "Why did you become sad Dad? Was it something that Kiran said that upset you?"

"No...nothing he said upset me, but I realized how much more useful I was to others in those years. And how dependent I am now on all of you. I am in no position to help anyone right now."

More tears flowed down his cheeks.

"Don't think like that Dad. You are sick now, but I am sure it is just a matter of time before you will be better, and then you can see about getting some kind of work to keep you busy. You know the pandemic has opened up so many remote working opportunities. I am sure there will be something that you can do."

"I don't know Archana...I can't even use a computer; how will I work remotely?"

"Learning to use a computer is nothing Dad; don't worry about that. I am sure we will be able to find a way, or maybe you can teach accounting concepts?" I said, trying to think of ways to make him feel better.

With all the trouble my dad was having with his mobility, I did not know how he would be able to work in the future, but I hoped that new treatments would be developed that could maybe cure Parkinson's and restore my dad's health.

"New treatments are being invented every day, Dad. I am sure very soon they will find something that can improve your health to what it was before Parkinson's. You just wait and see! I am sure the drug companies are working on finding a cure, and who knows, it may already be getting tested as we speak. Maybe it is just waiting for approval from the CDSCO; you never know."

I did not know whether Dad believed what I said, but I wanted to believe that a cure was possible in the near future, and I hoped that he believed it too. I had heard that since Parkinson's impacts the body's ability to produce dopamine, the ability to hope would have been seriously affected in my dad. But I hoped for some miracle so he could get better and do things for himself so he would at least not feel the way he did right now.

My mom and I wanted to so desperately see him healthy and happy; we prayed so much for that to happen.

Chapter 5 - Mr. Niyogi

"Mr. Niyogi..." I heard a voice while I was sleeping, and the voice woke me up. "Mr. Niyogi, please don't ignore me. Please help me."

"What?" I said, opening my eyes to find no one in the room. I was alone. It was the same voice that had come back to haunt me.

I needed to pee. "Manoj, can you come here?" I called out, "I need to go to the bathroom."

Manoj came into the room and brought me the urine bottle. I peed, and he left to throw it out into the toilet.

I never thought I would need someone else to help me even to pee. I never knew that I would have to depend on a caretaker like Manoj for things like that. I didn't know how long I could go on like this.

As soon as Manoj left the room, I started to drift back into sleep, and the voice was back.

"Mr. Niyogi, please do something. No one else is able to help us; it is only you who can help us," I heard the voice saying. It sounded like the voice was so close to my ear. I turned quickly in the direction of the sound only to see no one. There was no one else in the room, only me and this voice.

"Why...are you...bothering me," I whispered back to the voice, "I can't help you. I am bedridden. I can't even walk to the washroom to pee, let alone come to help you." I kept my voice down so I wouldn't come across as talking to myself and worrying others in the house.

"I heard you and your friend talking," the voice told me. "You used to work for Saran Airlines. I am sure Saran Airlines has a lot of money and resources to get a plane or a boat to the island where I am stuck. Please do something Mr. Niyogi. Please ask your former employer for help."

"I used to work there. I don't anymore," I whispered back. "I can't do anything to help now."

"I heard your friend saying that there is money missing from Saran's books," said the voice. "Maybe if you offer to help them find the money using your auditing skills, they may agree to send help over to the island to pick us up."

"What?" I countered, " that is crazy, I can't even step out of the house without so many people helping me out, what can I offer Saran Airlines when I have nothing to give?"

"Come on, Mr. Niyogi," implored the voice, "don't you believe that you have the skill and the experience to do the audit? I am sure there are very few people with the skills you have, plus you have a lot of history with Saran Airlines and know a lot about them."

"What are you saying?" I whispered back, "I can't ask my family to support me so I can go and do this work. They are already overstretched trying to keep me fed and helping me with my bathroom needs. I cannot ask more from them on top of everything they are doing for me. They know how weak and helpless I am. I am barely surviving. And how do you think I will be able to convince the folks at Saran Airlines to let me help them with this audit? And why would they even agree to help you in return? It all seems so absurd and stupid."

"It is easy for you to say all that Mr. Niyogi," said the voice, sounding sad. "You have all the help you need to get through your tough times, but unlike you, there is no one here to help us."

I did not respond, as I did not know what to say. The voice continued to talk to me, but I remained quiet. I was sure that the voice would lose hope and leave me alone, just like I had lost all hope of being normal again.

From the other room, I heard Ramani's voice; my lovely wife who had been with me every step of the way for the past fifty years. She was coming into the room to check on me.

"Hello dear," she said lovingly, "are you hungry? Do you want to eat something?"

"No..." I said, my voice raspy, as it had been lately, "I am not hungry. I don't want anything to eat...my left shoulder is in pain."

"Well, it is time to eat," she declared. "You are going to have something to eat, that's it."

"Manoj!" she called out, "can you bring the bowl of food that I left on the table?"

Manoj came in with the bowl along with the large syringe that he used to inject liquefied food into the feeding tube that ran to my stomach through my nose. While Ramani held my hand and sat with me, Manoj injected the food into the tube.

I could feel the warm liquid flowing down my feeding tube, but I could taste nothing, as the food completely bypassed my mouth. I had not tasted real food in some time, and I sorely missed being able to taste hot food and swallow it myself without having to depend on a feeding tube.

Before I got sick, Ramani was the one who needed more medical attention, but since I got sick with Parkinson's, there was no time for anyone to take care of Ramani at all, including herself. All of her—and everyone else's—attention and time went into taking care of my needs.

It was a lot on Ramani; she looked tired all the time. She used to read books and spend her spare time watching her favourite TV programs, but all of that was gone now. All that she ever did now was worry about me and do what she could to make sure I was as comfortable as possible.

I wish I could relieve her from her misery. At least for this reason, I couldn't wait for this disease to consume me so that I could leave and my family could move on with their lives. What could I do to get away from here? What could I do to give my family some rest so they could stop worrying about me?

After Manoj had finished injecting all the food into my feeding tube and left the room to clean the apparatus, I tapped Ramani's hand to get her attention.

"Yes dear," she asked, "what is it?"

"How are you doing? You are always taking care of me when I should be taking care of you."

"Don't worry about me, you have taken care of me a lot. Now I am temporarily taking care of you. I am sure you will be better soon, and you will be taking care of me again while I spend my time watching my TV serials."

"I don't know if I will ever be normal again, Ramani. I don't even remember normal. Day after day, I am becoming more and more dependent on you and everyone else."

"Look my dear, stop worrying about that. You should have hope, and you should focus on getting rest and getting better."

"Hmm." I did not know what else to say; I did not know what to think. *Will I be of use to anyone at all? Maybe there is something that I can do. Maybe I can help this boy somehow, the son of Archana's friend, Rajamouli. If I am of use to no one else, maybe I can at least try to help this boy.*

I knew it was a long shot. What could I offer Saran Airlines that would make them send help to a faraway island to help people they were not connected to at all?

Well, what did I have to lose? I would ask if I could help and see if they accepted. If they did accept, I would ask and see if they were willing to help with the rescue. If they didn't agree, I had nothing to lose. If they did agree, I could at least hope to get that voice to stop bothering me day in and day out.

I touched Ramani's hand again and said, "I want to talk to Kiran Singh again…I felt very good the other day after meeting with him. I want to talk to him again.''

"Okay dear, I will tell Archana to call Kiran again," she said and got up to leave the room.

Later that evening when Archana came over, my Ramani must have told her about my request. After a while, Archana came into the room and said that Kiran would come visit the following weekend. She said that Kiran told her they were dealing with a crisis at work, so he could not come immediately.

Kiran did not show that weekend, but he came over two weeks later. He was his usual cheerful self when he came in, and I dragged myself to the living room again to talk with him.

"Hello Mr. Niyogi," he said cheerily, "it is so good to see you again. How have you been? I am so sorry I could not come earlier, sir."

"I am doing okay…" I managed to say, "how are you?"

We spoke for some time about his family. After a while, Ramani and Archana went into the kitchen, and only Kiran and I remained in the living room. I beckoned for Kiran to lean forward and I said, "I need your help with something."

"Yes sir, anything," he said, sounding concerned.

"I need you to tell Mr. Saran that I can help him with his audit and help track the money the company seems to be missing," I said, straining hard to keep my voice low and coherent. "I can help, but I can't let my family know about this. I don't want to burden them any more than I already do."

"Why do you want to take the trouble at all, sir?" Kiran asked, not understanding why I was trying to take this on. "You are still recovering from Parkinson's; why do you want to put more strain on yourself?"

"I don't know why Kiran," I said, continuing to keep my voice down, which was not that hard, as my voice was barely audible after getting this disease, "but I have a strong feeling that I must do this. I have to do this."

"But why sir?" Kiran sounded annoyed. "Your whole family is taking care of you, and you need so much support to manage your day-to-day activities. Why do you want to take on this work? Won't it be a lot of trouble for you to do this work while you manage your pain or other discomforts that you are experiencing?"

"Maybe you are right," I said, dejected. "Maybe I should just not worry about this and try to relax. This incurable disease has left me feeling so hollow and helpless. I am of no use to anyone. I want to be useful to someone at least. I know it may sound stupid, but I want you to think about it and help me by trying to find out if Mr. Saran will agree to me helping with the audit. Will you please think about it?"

"Okay sir," said Kiran, not sounding sure, "I will think about this and get back you."

"Please remember Kiran," I said, taking a look to make sure that my wife and daughter were still too far away to hear me, "I don't want my family to know. They cannot know about this."

Kiran left soon after, and I went back to my usual routine. I did not hear back from Kiran for the next two weeks. My days were filled with sleeping, consuming pureed food through my feeding tube, waiting for my body pains to torture me repeatedly, multiple times each day, and consuming what felt like a hundred pills a day.

One of the side effects of the medication I was taking was constipation. As if what I was going through was not enough, the constipation made my life even harder. I couldn't eat food properly, and my body could not get rid of it easily. It was hell.

The third week after Kiran's visit, Archana came over and said that Kiran had called and asked if he could come to see me again. I could not let Archana know that I was waiting eagerly for him to get back to me. I nodded to let her know that I was okay with that.

A couple of days later, Kiran came over in the morning. He came in, sat down in the living room and waited for me to amble over to the chair next to him.

After the common pleasantries, when he and I were alone in the room, he said that he had spoken to Mr. Saran about my idea. "Mr. Saran also thinks it is a stupid idea for you to try to tackle this audit, given your condition, but he is desperate and needs to resolve this issue soon. Given that the company has grown much larger than when you were working there, and because the organization now has many more transport divisions, he does not think that you will be able to find the missing money, but he is willing to give it a try.

"So, he said that he can give you one week to find the money. Oh, and one more thing, he wanted to meet with you first before the work starts. What do you think about that sir?"

"Oh, one week is all I get?" I asked, feeling dejected already. How could I find the money in one week? My ability to sit and read something had deteriorated terribly. I couldn't even hold a pen, let alone write something legibly. How could I do this in one week? Should I stop this madness and let it be? But I was the one who asked for this opportunity, how could I back out now? "Okay, let me at least give it a shot. The challenge now is to try and do this without my family finding out. Can you give me some time, maybe a few weeks, so I can try to arrange something to make it work?"

"Yes sir, sure, take all the time that you need," said Kiran, "and if after thinking it over you decide that this is too much and you can't handle it, that is fine too." Kiran sounded like he would have much preferred it if I dropped this completely.

After he left, I went back to recover in my bed. Kiran might have thought that I would be doing him a favour by giving up the idea altogether.

I understood why he might feel like this. It was going to be a lot of work for someone to feed me, help me with my bathroom needs and provide me with all the things I would need to do this work, given my failing physical abilities.

How could I still make it happen, and above all else, how could I do this without my family knowing about it? How was I going to escape their gaze and get away from the house for a week so I could do this work? Could I even pull it off in one week? When I was at my best, I might have been able to do something like this in one week, but now I was feeling less than confident that I could even make a dent in one week. Nonetheless, I had to try. I had to give it a shot.

I couldn't work on a computer, so I would have to work on paper, which meant that Kiran would have to bring printouts of everything. That way, I'd be able to read, make my notes and write out what had to be done.

Who can help me do this? Mr. Saran wants to see me first, and I have already asked a lot from Kiran. Who can help me pull this off?

Chapter 6 - Muthuswamy

Niyogi and I used to be in the Lions Club of Sagar. We used to work very well together in the club. Niyogi was a kind person who never disparaged anyone. He always focused on how to solve problems rather than finding reasons to complain and nag about them. He did not have very many friends, but I did. To this day I still have a huge list of people I can count on as my friends and who I can expect help from if I need it, because I have helped them in the past. There is not one area in which I don't have a friend or two that owes me a favour.

After I retired from my job at the electronics factory, I was asked to manage the convention hall that belonged to the factory. I have been at it for a few years now, and I am enjoying it. I have no reason to stop. Although Niyogi is no longer part of the club, I still am. I want to do my part to contribute to this world as best as I can.

The other day I was in the hospital for my annual checkup when I saw Niyogi with his daughter. Niyogi was in a wheelchair. He looked so worn down and weak compared to the active and lively person he used to be when we were in the club together. In addition to being the treasurer of the club, he was also the Tail Twister and used to tell jokes between meetings. Not all of his jokes landed, but he tried his best.

"Hello Niyogi," I said, walking up to them, "how are you? So nice to see you after such a long time. And Archana, how are you my dear?"

"I am doing well Uncle, how are you?" said Archana while Niyogi looked at me with a smile and waved. I went closer and took Niyogi's hand to shake it. His grip was so weak.

"Good to know Archana. Nice to see you," I said. Then, looking at Niyogi, I asked, "And Niyogi, how come you are at the hospital?"

"Parkinson's," whispered Niyogi, and then he cleared his throat and repeated a little more loudly, "Parkinson's. I've had it for a couple of years, Muthu. I am not the same as I was before."

"What are you talking about?" I said, not wanting to show the sadness that I felt seeing Niyogi like this. "You look as good as ever. Come, let's go for a coffee; I hear the hospital cafeteria has excellent coffee."

"Okay, I will come," said Niyogi. I was not expecting him to say yes, but I was glad that he agreed to come.

"Okay, what time does your appointment end?" I asked.

"We are seeing the doctor in fifteen minutes," said Archana. "We should be done in an hour or so."

"Okay, great!" I said. "I will be back right here in an hour, and we'll go to the cafeteria for a coffee, okay?"

"Okay, see you," said Niyogi, trying to smile.

"Yes Uncle, see you soon," Archana said.

I started to walk away, and I could hear Archana tell Niyogi, "So nice of him, right Dad? It has been so long..."

Through my work with the Lion's Club, I often went to the hospital to organize blood donation camps, and sometimes, I would bring blood collected from donation camps conducted elsewhere. So, I have a lot of contacts at the hospital. I spent the next hour meeting some people and preparing for a few blood donation camps that were coming up in the coming months.

As the hour was ending, I went back to the same spot where I had seen

Niyogi and his daughter earlier. They were not there yet, so I waited for fifteen minutes or so. Eventually I could see Niyogi being brought out of a room in his wheelchair by his daughter. I waved to them and walked over. Archana told me that she needed to go and collect some medication from the pharmacy, and she asked if I could take Niyogi to the cafeteria. She would meet us there.

So, Archana went in the direction of the pharmacy, and I got behind Niyogi's wheelchair and pushed him towards the cafeteria. I found an empty table and moved a chair to make way for Niyogi's wheelchair. Then I went and sat down across from him.

"So, Niyogi, what would you like to have, coffee or tea? Oh, wait, I remember you always used to drink coffee," I said, rising to get a couple of coffees for us.

Niyogi raised his hand and called me closer. "Sorry Muthu, because of this feeding tube, I can't drink coffee like normal. It has to be through the tube...difficult here and now. You get coffee for yourself." Niyogi's voice was raspy and barely louder than a whisper.

"Oh, sorry Niyogi, I did not notice that. I am not very thirsty right now; I will drink coffee later," I said and sat down on a chair closer to him. "Well, you will get better soon Niyogi, I know it," I said, trying to sound cheerful. "You can join the club again once you are better."

"I don't know Muthu. I feel I am very far from getting better right now," said Niyogi, weakly holding on to the table with his hands for support. "I am dependent on everyone for everything."

"Niyogi, you know I am always honest with you, right? I want to say, you should not have left the club," I told him. "I always believed that retirement is the number one killer of old people."

"You may be right there Muthu," said Niyogi. "On that note, I am glad I ran into you today. I wanted to ask you for some help. I need to do something, but I don't want my family to know about it."

I was intrigued. What was it that Niyogi wanted to do?

"Sure, friend, I am always ready to help you," I said. "Tell me what you need."

"I need to visit my ex-employer at his office in Kalasipalyam. And I need someone to take me there without my family knowing that I went there."

"Can I ask why you want to do this Niyogi?" I asked, curious to know why Niyogi wanted to do such a thing while also excited at the prospect of such an intriguing challenge.

"Well, it is something that I want to do," said Niyogi. "I am so fed up with depending on everyone for everything, I feel so useless. I want do something meaningful; I want to be useful to someone at least."

"Why don't you want your family to know what you are trying to do?"

"I am worried that they may discourage me from doing this because of their concern for my health," Niyogi said.

"Are you planning to ask for your old job back?"

"No, but I know that I can help the company with a problem they have been having recently. I want to pitch the idea to my ex-boss."

"Are you sure that is a good idea? You cannot even walk by yourself, friend."

"I know...but I still have to try. You know there is no cure for Parkinson's. Things are only going to get worse for me from now on. There is no getting better for me."

"I still think it is a stupid idea, Niyogi," I said. I could see Niyogi's expression turn sad. "You know what? Let me think about this and I will get back to you. I will call you and let you know if it is possible."

"Call my daughter and ask her to give the phone to me. And try to keep things vague when we speak, okay?"

"Okay, I will let you know. I still think..." Just then I saw Archana walking towards us. "Okay, your daughter is here." I got up and shook Niyogi's hand.

"Take care friend, I will call you sometime," I said loudly so that

Archana would hear me. "Oh Archana, just in time, I was about to leave. It was so nice talking to Niyogi after all this time. Listen, if I wanted to talk to Niyogi on the phone, can I call you?"

"Yes Uncle Muthu, of course you can call me," said Archana. She bent down to Niyogi and asked him if he was ready to go home. Niyogi nodded. He looked at me before Archana turned the wheelchair around and slowly started wheeling him away.

During our days together at the club, Niyogi was always ready to join me whenever some work needed to be done. He never once shied away from work, however hard it seemed. We spent many days together on the road as we travelled to remote villages to organize blood donation camps, cataract surgery camps or food donation drives. I wanted to help him; I just did not know how.

If he was dependent on his family for everything and couldn't even travel somewhere alone, how could I secretly take him to his ex-employer's office in Kalasipalyam? It seemed too far-fetched to accomplish something like that. I had to get going, so I put that thought aside and went about my day.

Later that night, I kept wondering if it was wise for me to help Niyogi with doing what he wanted to do. Was that what was best for him? Finally, I decided that Parkinson's or not, Niyogi was my friend, and he was trying to do something in his life, something no one expected him to do. But he wanted to do it anyway, and I would help him in whatever way I could.

Having come to that decision, I now had to figure out how to help him. He did not use his phone himself anymore; his wife had it. So direct communication with him was not possible. I would have to go through his daughter. But how could I do that and still convey something to him that he alone could understand?

Before I started worrying about how to convey things to him, I needed to figure out how to get him to Kalasipalyam. From his house, it would take about an hour to get there. Let's say he'd need an hour to meet with his ex-boss and another hour or hour and a half to get back. So in total, I needed to get him away for about four hours without anyone finding out.

Archana was at work during the day, but his wife would be there. So, if this meeting was planned for some time between 10 a.m. and 5 p.m., we would have to find a way to distract his wife for four hours.

Maybe I could arrange a fake celebration in Niyogi's honour at the club? I could go get him with a car full of people and tell his wife that I only have room for him and his wheelchair, and that I will bring him back in four hours.

That would be a good excuse for Niyogi to get dressed up to make the best possible impression on his ex-boss. Well, at least he could try to make the best possible impression.

With a plan taking shape, I was able to sleep that night. The first thing I had to do was to call up Archana and somehow get the message to Niyogi that I would take him to meet with his ex-boss.

The next day, I waited until evening and called Archana at around 6 p.m.

"Hello Archana, this is Muthuswamy. How are you doing?" I said once she answered the phone.

"I am doing well Uncle, how are you?" said Archana, sounding a bit puzzled about why I was calling her.

"I am doing well dear. Hey listen, after I met your dad yesterday, I was speaking with others in the club, and they all want to throw him a celebration. Sort of like an award ceremony for all his contributions to the club and the community. It will be a small affair, just four or five of us."

"Oh, that is very nice of you Uncle," said Archana, "but I am not sure how it will be possible, as you know my dad has a lot of difficulty moving around, and since he got Parkinson's, he has become very reluctant to see people. I am not sure how easy this is going to be."

"Ah, I see…I understand. Well, I will take care of taking him to the event and bringing him back home. As for him being comfortable with it, let me talk to him and see if I can convince him."

"Okay Uncle, I will give the phone to him. You can try to convince him," said Archana. "I am putting the phone on speaker. Now you can talk, and my father will hear you."

"Hello Niyogi, how are you?" I said.

"I am fine Muthu," I heard Niyogi's feeble voice saying.

"Okay friend. I want to tell you something, and I want you to agree to it, okay? Look, some folks at the club want to throw you a party for all the work you have done for the club when you were a member. You don't have to worry about anything; I will take you to the event. I want you to agree to come."

"Did you hear that Dad?" I heard Archana saying. "They want to give you an award. You should go Dad!"

"Hmm, I am not sure Muthu…I am not in any way in a presentable state. I don't know how the other folks will take it, and I don't know if I can handle it."

"Oh, come on. It will be a very short event; you will be in and out in an hour tops."

"No…Muthu, I can't…" I heard Niyogi say.

Does he not understand why I am calling him? I thought. *I don't think he remembers what he asked me to do yesterday. I have to find a way to tell him without alerting his daughter.*

"No, don't say that! It will be fun; there will be some important people who will be attending. You will surely want to meet them. Yesterday when we spoke you said you wanted to meet all the important people." *I hope he gets it now at least.*

"Uh…okay, I will come. When is it?" asked Niyogi, his reluctance still apparent in his voice.

"Very soon. I will arrange everything and let Archana know the date, okay? You just be ready, and I will do the rest."

"Okay...thank you Muthu," said Niyogi.

"Archana dear?"

"Yes Uncle?"

"I will call you once the date is finalized and all the details have been ironed out. Please make sure that your dad does not change his mind."

"Yes Uncle. I will do my best. Thank you once again Uncle, this is very nice of you."

"You are most welcome my dear. Bye now," I said and hung up.

I really hope Niyogi remembers what he asked of me yesterday and realizes that this is in fact to help him meet with his ex-boss. Now I have to start planning this; we have to make it look like there is an actual celebration. We'll need to take pictures that Niyogi can show his family. And I will need to call his ex-boss and try to make an appointment. I am sure Niyogi is in no state to book an appointment by himself.

Chapter 7 - Mr. Niyogi

His face was covered with black soot, except where his tears had left two river-like paths down from his eyes. His hands were shaking, he was on his knees and looking at me pleadingly.

"Mr. Niyogi," he was saying, "please do not forget about us. Are you doing anything to help us?"

"I told you already, I cannot help you," I said to him.

"Please Mr. Niyogi, please, please, please, PLEASE, PLEASE, PLEASE, PLEASE, BEEP, BEEP, BEEP..."

I woke up to the sound of the alarm. It was coming from my phone next to the bed; well, it used to be my phone. Now it was mine and Ramani's.

I looked around to see if the boy was still there, the boy who had been bothering me so much the last few weeks. With a sigh of relief, I let my head fall back on the pillow. There was no one in the room except Ramani, who had just walked in to turn off the alarm.

"It's time to get up dear, you need to start getting ready for your event at the club," she said.

Today was the "party" that Muthu had planned. I was truly hoping that the party was but a ruse to get me out of the house so I could go and meet Mr. Saran. I really hoped that Muthu had pulled it off.

"Can you remove the feeding tube?" I asked Ramani, "I don't want to look ridiculous with a feeding tube in the photos. I will have my breakfast, and then you can remove the tube and put it back after I return."

"Oh dear, what if you get hungry before you are back? How will you have anything without the tube? What about water?"

"I won't need it; I won't be out for that long. I don't want the tube when I see those people."

"Okay fine, I will ask Manoj to remove it," she said and called out to Manoj, "Manoj, can you come here?"

Manoj came in with a basin and a small stool along with my toothbrush, toothpaste and a towel. He helped me brush my teeth and then helped me take a shower. He also helped me with taking a shit. Once all of that was done, he told Ramani that I was ready for breakfast.

Ramani brought in my liquefied breakfast in a bowl, and then Manoj helped with injecting it into the feeding tube.

"Manoj, can you also remove the tube once his breakfast is done? He has an event to go to today, and he does not want the tube," said Ramani.

"Yes madam, I will remove it. We can put a new one in once Mr. Niyogi is back home after the event."

Manoj then slowly pulled out the tube through my nose. I had to hold on tight to the edge of the bed to keep myself still. Once it was out, I felt such relief. As much as I depended on the tube for my survival, I was glad to be rid of it, even if it was just for a short while.

Manoj then helped me get into an adult diaper, a pair of formal trousers and a button-down shirt, a belt for the trousers, and finally my slip-on shoes. It felt like a million years ago that I used to wear these clothes six days a week when I was working and active, when there was no sign of this sickness that had crippled me.

I waddled to the bathroom one last time and after I was done got help from Manoj to pull the diaper and the pants back up, knowing that I would have to manage with the diaper for the next three to four hours. There was no going back now. I had to get through this; I had to find a way to convince Mr. Saran to let me work on the audit. And most of all, I had to get to Kalasipalyam and back with all my bodily fluids under control. There was no way I could even get a sip of water until I was back and the feeding tube was reinserted.

I suddenly felt dizzy. I did not know if I could do this. I was so nervous; I could feel sweat forming in my armpits and on my forehead.

Ramani came into the room. She took one look at me, and I could see her hesitance to let me go through with this.

"My dear, are you sure you are up for this?" she asked, wiping away the sweat from my forehead with the end of her cotton sari. "Wouldn't it be better if you do this over a video call or something instead of you actually going there?"

She looked at Manoj to see if he had anything to say, and he nodded at her, indicating that he agreed.

Just then the doorbell rang. Ramani went to the door and came back to the bedroom with Muthu. Muthu looked me up and down; he also looked unsure about this whole thing.

"Mr. Muthu?" said Ramani, "do you really think it is essential for my husband to come with you? Can't this be done over a video call or something?"

"Ah, Ramani, I see that you are nervous about this. But let me assure you, it is very important that Niyogi is there in person for this celebration to thank him for everything he has done for the club and for the people that our club serves. I am sure it will be fine; we have two nurses and a doctor in the club who will be attending today's event. I am sure they can step in and help if needed."

The confidence in Muthu's voice reassured Ramani a little bit, and she asked me once more to make sure, "Are you sure you want to go?"

I did not want to look anyone in the eye, lest they see how uncertain I was feeling.

"I can manage, I will manage. Muthu...let's go," I said and turned my head towards the door, not even looking at Muthu.

Ramani asked Manoj to bring the wheelchair, and they both helped me get into the chair, putting my feet up on the foot pedestals.

I looked at the clock to make a note of the time. It was 10 a.m. I had to be back by 2 p.m. at the latest. *Let's go Niyogi, it's now or never.*

With what looked like a lot of reluctance, Ramani let me go with Muthu. Muthu pushed my wheelchair to the elevator and then to his car. I stood up and got into the front seat with his help. My throat was already parched, but I couldn't do anything about it. Muthu folded my wheelchair and put it in the trunk, got into the driver's seat and started driving.

He waited until we were outside of the apartment complex before he said, "I have already called Mr. Saran and booked an appointment with him. We are going straight to his office."

"Thank you...Muthu," I said, having difficulty speaking as my throat dried up. As much as I wanted this, I was extremely nervous.

What am I going to say to Mr. Saran? How am I even going to convince him to let me work on finding his missing money? Is he going to call me crazy and ask me to get lost?

The drive to Kalasipalyam took more than an hour, and the closer we got to the office, the more I was sweating. I tried to distract myself by looking at the traffic on the road; the traffic that I used to be a regular part of many years ago. Muthu's car turned onto KR Road and then VVI Road. Finally, he stopped in front of the Saran Airlines offices.

"We are here Niyogi," said Muthu, getting out of the car and coming around to my side to open the door for me.

I couldn't move. I froze; I couldn't even turn my head towards the office.

"I can't...I can't go...I want to go back home..." I was saying, but it was barely audible to Muthu.

He leaned closer to try and hear what I was mumbling. I was too afraid to say to him that I wanted to go back home, and I was too afraid to get out of the car to go and meet Mr. Saran.

Either Muthu did not notice the struggle I was going through, or he chose not to notice it. He quickly ran to the back of his car to get the wheelchair out. He opened the door, leaned in and unhooked the seat belt. He then held out his hand for me to take to get out of the seat. I complied. I did not have the strength to say anything to the contrary.

Muthu helped me to stand up and supported me as I shuffled my feet towards the chair and slumped into it. Muthu then locked the car and wheeled me to the main lobby. He spoke to the receptionist, and she asked us to wait a few minutes.

I had my head down and I was shaking, saying to myself that I could not do this. Muthu wheeled me to the waiting area and sat next to me in a chair. He then leaned closer to me and said, "For a second I was not sure you wanted to get out of the car, friend. I had to move around a lot of things to do this for you. You came here to do something that you wanted to do, so do what you came here to do."

I turned towards him, and he gave me an encouraging thumbs-up and patted my back. There was no way I could back out now. I had to go through with it. I took a deep breath and started planning what to say to Mr. Saran.

After around fifteen minutes of waiting, Mr. Saran's secretary came over and said that Mr. Saran was ready to see us. Muthu quickly got up and wheeled me towards Mr. Saran's office. We were behind the secretary as he walked ahead of us. The double doors to Mr. Saran's office were open, and he was standing at the door waiting for us. As soon as he saw me, he paused with a look of mild shock at my appearance. Even though Kiran had told him about me, I don't think he had any idea of the changes Parkinson's had caused in me.

He recovered quickly and stepped forward to shake my hand. He held my weak outstretched hand with both of his and said, "It is so nice to see you Niyogi, how have you been?"

"I am doing fine," I said weakly, "as fine as I can be at least. How are you Mr. Saran?"

"Oh, I am doing great, as you can see," he said, waving his hand from his head to his toes. "Kiran told me he saw you and that you wanted to talk to me. How is your family doing? Mrs. Niyogi and your daughter, are they doing well?"

"Yes, they are doing well, thank you," I said. "This is my friend Muthuswamy."

"Nice to meet you Mr. Muthuswamy."

"Nice to meet you Mr. Saran. I will let you both talk; I will be outside." Muthu ensured that the wheels of my chair were locked and then walked out, closing the door behind him.

"So, tell me Niyogi, what can I do for you?" asked Mr. Saran, walking to his chair and sitting down. I could see a giant poster of a fleet of aircraft behind him, all bearing the Saran Airlines logo.

"Mr. Saran, Kiran told me about the audit that you have going on. He did not tell me much, but I wanted to offer my services to help you with the audit."

"Oh, that is interesting, and I can surely use your help on this one," said Mr. Saran, bringing his hands together with his fingers touching at the tips, "but tell me Niyogi, aren't you sick? I see that you need a wheelchair to move around. How much would you be able to do? And besides, why do you want to trouble yourself at this age with your health issues?"

"Since I retired, I've been at home, first taking care of my family, Mr. Saran, and now they are taking care of me. I feel like I have become a burden on them. I want to contribute in some way to help someone, and company finance is something I was good at, as you very well know."

"Yes, that is true indeed. You were the best internal auditor and accountant I ever had," said Mr. Saran, still not fully convinced. "But with your failing health, do you still think you will be able to work?"

"I will admit that I can't write anymore, but I still read and do a lot of things in my head," I said, trying my best to sound more confident than I felt. "And besides, I am sure there are some aspects of this audit that can benefit from someone like me, who knows the company so well."

"That is true; there are some aspects of this audit that my team is struggling with, and I can't bring in external auditors for this, since it involves confidential company data that I am not comfortable sharing with just anybody.

"But, when Kiran came to me saying that you wanted to work for me again, and when he suggested that we bring you in on this particular audit, I was not sure. And now, after seeing you, I feel even more strongly that you may be over straining yourself if you take this on. Are you sure you are up for this?"

I had to pause before answering him. I looked at the poster behind him once more, and in addition to all the aircraft, I also saw a few of ocean liners and passenger ships.

"I understand why you are hesitating," I said, "and I have to admit that it will not be easy for me to work again...but more than anything else, I want to contribute to the world in some way. I want to be able to give something to someone before this disease takes any more of me. I will put in every bit of energy that I have and do my part for this audit. In return, you can give me money that I can pass on to my family, or you can think of it as a favour and return the favour some other way; it's up to you."

"I hear you Niyogi. I see that you don't want to give up without a fight. I respect that. Help me find confidence in you again. Why don't you do a small task for me first, and then if you are able to do it, I will let you work on the rest of the audit. Is that okay?"

"Yes, thank you very much...I really appreciate this," I said, feeling much better. "I have one condition. I don't want my family to know that I am doing this. If they find out, they will not let me do it out of concern for my health. I will need certain accommodations so I can do this work without them coming to know about it."

"Okay sure. Kiran and I will do our best to accommodate you because of all the work that you have done for me in the past and how you have helped grow this company. I must leave for a meeting now, Niyogi. It was great seeing you, and I look forward to you helping us with this audit. See you soon."

Mr. Saran then picked up the phone on his desk and told his secretary to ask Muthu to come in. Muthu soon came into the room and thanked Mr. Saran for his time. He unlocked the wheels of my chair and wheeled me out of the room and towards the main entrance of the building.

As scared as I was before going to see Mr. Saran, I was now consumed by how I was going to do everything I had promised to do. I had been holding my pee for some time, and while Muthu was wheeling me to the car, I peed in my diaper. I hoped that nothing would spill out of the diaper and cause any discomfort to Muthu.

He then helped me get into his car, folded and placed my wheelchair in the back of the car and checked his watch. It had been two hours and forty-five minutes since we left home. My throat was still parched, but I couldn't do anything about it because I was not sure I could even drink water without my feeding tube.

Muthu got into the driver's seat beside me and handed me a memento with my name on it, thanking me for all my contributions to the club.

"This is your 'award' Niyogi. I am going to say that in the excitement to see you, we forgot to take pictures at the celebration. Let's get you home so you can get some food in you if you are hungry."

"Thank you once again Muthu, you are a great friend," I said.

"It's okay my friend, you can thank me later. I need to hurry and get you back home now." With that, he pulled away from the curb and focused on driving me back home as fast as he could. All the while, I was thinking what I should do next. How could I do this work without my family knowing?

Chapter 8 - Mr. Niyogi

Three days after the meeting with Mr. Saran, Kiran visited me. Manoj was off that day; Archana was busy with some extra work she had to do, and Ramani was the only one at home. After Ramani let Kiran in, she came into my room to take me to the living room. I shuffled over to the living room with her help to sit down beside Kiran, and then Ramani left to make coffee for him.

After spending a few minutes talking about nothing in particular, Kiran lowered his voice so that Ramani would not hear and asked me, "Mr. Niyogi, when do you want to start the work?"

"The sooner the better," I whispered back, "every day I feel like it is becoming more and more difficult to move around."

Kiran put a compassionate hand on my shoulder and nodded.

"How do we do this?"

"I have been wondering the same. I have spent three days thinking about how I can get away from the house," I said.

"Do you go to any physiotherapy or regular medical appointments?"

"I don't on a regular basis; I go as needed...but maybe I should. That would give me a good excuse to get out of the house," I said, thinking out loud.

"Okay then, let me look for something near the office. Maybe you can pop by the office after or before your therapy sessions and get a chance to do some work."

"Kiran, I am too embarrassed...to come into the office every day, the way I am...I don't know how people will take it if I come in with a feeding tube hanging from my nose."

"Hmm," said Kiran, his hand on his chin, "there is a physiotherapy center in the same complex as my cousin's dance studio. Maybe you can go there for therapy and stop by the dance studio afterwards? I could bring some documents for you to read there."

"Okay, give me the address and I will ask Archana to look into it. Can you recommend the clinic to Ramani so she can talk to Archana?"

Right on cue, Ramani came into the living room with a coffee for herself and Kiran. She sat down next to me.

"Raman ma'am, my father told this to me the other day, and it might help Niyogi sir too. My father's cousin is also suffering from Parkinson's, and he said that his pain became more manageable with physiotherapy. Have you considered arranging physiotherapy for Mr. Niyogi?"

"He had some physio a while back, but it did not help much," she said, not wanting to dismiss Kiran completely.

"Maybe there are certain specific types of therapy that are designed to help Parkinson's patients. I will give you the address of this place; please call them tomorrow and ask what programs they have specifically for Parkinson's patients. I will get their phone number and share it with Archana tomorrow. Please give them a call; it might help Mr. Niyogi a lot."

Later that day when Archana came over, Ramani told her about what Kiran had said regarding the therapy center. Archana turned to me and asked, "Dad, do you want to go and try this therapy? Three months ago when we asked, you said you did not want to go to therapy. Kiran is saying this is very helpful; do you want to try it?"

"I don't know...maybe let's try it," I said.

"What do you think Mummy?" Archana asked Ramani.

"Well, if your dad is willing to try it, why not?"

"Okay, I will call the clinic and see what options they have for Parkinson's patients."

A couple of days passed before Archana said anything else about the clinic.

"Hey Dad," she called, walking into my room, "you know what, the clinic said they have a few options that we can try. I have booked an appointment with them for the coming Thursday in the evening. We will go then, okay?"

"Okay," I said.

Some days my Parkinson's medicine worked and I was able to speak better, but on other days the medicine was not all that effective. That was one of those days. I had trouble speaking. I gestured for Archana to come closer, and she leaned closer to me.

"Tell...Kiran...that we are going to try the clinic...he may want to know..." I managed to say with much difficulty.

"Oh, don't worry about that. I already told him and thanked him. I am hoping for something good to come out of it."

So am I my dear, so am I.

I still did not know how I was going to meet up with Kiran and work with him on the audit. How was I going to get to this dance studio he talked about? Who could I ask to take me there? I had already asked so much from Kiran, and he would have to do so much more to help me do this work while hiding it all from Archana and Ramani. Ever since getting this wretched ailment, I had lost contact with all my friends. I could only talk to anyone with help from either Ramani or Archana, and sometimes I couldn't focus long enough to be able to talk and explain something.

How long could I really carry on this clandestine activity without them finding out and stopping me from doing it? Was it really worth all this trouble; to risk upsetting them and giving them more to worry about? I was not really worried about failing to do the job that I had offered to do. I had nothing to lose. It wasn't like I would lose my job if I couldn't do what I had promised. And I would be gone in a few years anyway, so I didn't care if Mr. Saran thought that I wasted his time. But I was worried about what would happen to Kiran. He was risking his reputation by helping me...

That Thursday evening, Archana took me and Ramani to the clinic. It was a large clinic that offered many kinds of treatment and therapy. We were asked to meet Dr. Surendra Reddy. Dr. Reddy was a specialist dealing with Parkinson's and other neurological disorders. We went into his office and waited for him to come and see me. Archana had brought the reports of all the tests I had done so far. The binder with the reports was three inches thick. Ramani was sitting to my left, Archana to my right.

After we had waited for fifteen minutes, the door on the right opened, and in walked Dr. Reddy. He was a short man no more than thirty-five years old. He had a receding hairline, and he looked tired with dark circles around his eyes.

"Hello, good evening. How can I help you today?" he said as he sat down in his chair.

"Hello doctor, we are here today regarding my father," said Archana, gesturing towards me. "He was diagnosed with Parkinson's three years ago and has been on medication since then. A friend of ours told us about your clinic and said that you may have some therapy that could help Parkinson's patients. We are here to learn more and see if you have anything that can help my father. "

"Okay, I understand. Well, it is nice to meet you all," said Dr. Reddy, looking at all three of us. "Do you have any reports that I could look at to better understand your father's condition?"

Archana handed him the binder, and he started going through the more recent reports. He flipped through the reports for a good ten minutes, saying nothing but a few "hmms" while holding his chin with the fingers of his right hand. It looked like his left hand was the dominant one.

Once he was done reading the reports, he asked what medication I was taking. Archana said that I was talking Syndopa CR and Syndopa Plus.

"I am sure you must be experiencing the side effects of those medications?" he asked, looking at me.

I nodded. "Yes doctor."

"Okay, here is what I can offer you. We offer two types of therapy for Parkinson's patients. As you know, Parkinson's affects the body's natural dopamine-producing ability, and there is no cure for it yet. What we can do is find ways to make the body release dopamine, which can help you temporarily by improving your day-to-day activities. Muscular control, strength, energy levels, and even mood could improve temporarily while the dopamine produced by the body lasts.

"I strongly believe, and it has been proven time and time again, that the body, the brain and the nervous system are all interconnected. Much like being happy can make someone smile and laugh, the physical act of smiling and laughing can cause the body to actually experience an increased level of happiness or joy in that moment. On the same lines, a healthy level of dopamine in the body can propel someone to start doing physical activity, and physical activity can trigger a release of dopamine in the body.

"So, the first type of therapy that we can offer will be to make Mr. Niyogi do some physical activity, as per his abilities, and force his endocrine system to generate dopamine. The therapy's level of success varies from patient to patient. Everyone responds differently. We can only try and see how Mr. Niyogi responds."

"My father's ability to engage in physical activity has diminished greatly, doctor. Could this really work for him?"

"Like I said, we have to try and see. The results really vary from person to person."

Archana and Ramani were listening to what the doctor was saying with great interest.

"And what is the second type of therapy you would recommend?" asked Ramani.

"The second is a more recent development and requires some specialized equipment. It involves stimulating the patient with electrical impulses to certain points on the spine. These impulses will then kick start a flurry of communication within his neurological system and leave him energized and active."

"Are they electrical shocks?" asked Archana, sounding spooked by the images the phrase "electrical impulses" might have triggered in her mind.

"I know what you are thinking, and this is not that," clarified Dr. Reddy. "The impulses are very low voltage, no more than 1.5 volts, much like the voltage from a small triple-A battery. We place around seven to nine connectors on the patient's spine, and we then administer a sequence of impulses, which in turn triggers the heightened activity in the nervous system."

"How long...will the effects of the...therapy last?" I asked, working hard for each word to be audible enough for the doctor to hear.

"Well, like I said, the results vary from person to person," he said. "In some of our best cases, the physical therapy showed a significant improvement for up to three days. We won't know what the improvement will be exactly until we try it on you though, because like I said, the results vary drastically. The electrical stimulation has shown a significantly better response, but the effects have only lasted for a day. We have seen patients who received the electrical therapy finding it easy to stand up and walk, talk effortlessly and even write."

"Oh wow," said Archana, visibly excited at the prospect of seeing improvement in my condition. Her excitement was contagious, which Ramani must have felt too, as she had a wide smile on her face.

Could this really help me do the work that I want to do?

"Are there any side effects? If we decide to go ahead with it...is there any danger of detrimental long-term effects?" asked Archana.

"Both of these types of therapy have not been around for long; we have only been offering it to our patients for the past two years. So, I personally have not had enough time to study the long-term effects, but the research that has already been published has shown that people can become over-dependent on the electrical stimulation if we are not careful and we don't space it out."

"So, we really have to consider whether the short-term benefits of this therapy are worth the longer-term risks?" asked Archana, looking at me and Ramani in turn.

"Yes. Please do take some time to think it through. We can proceed with the therapy if you want to go ahead. For today though, I can offer a complimentary fifteen-minute therapy session at a low intensity to see if Mr. Niyogi likes it. Do you want to try that out?"

The doctor seemed eager to sign us up for the therapy. I also wanted to find out if it would really work for me.

Before Archana or Ramani could say no, I said, "Yes, I want to try."

Archana and Ramani exchanged looks. They turned to the doctor and Archana shrugged.

"Okay, that is great! Let's get this going," said Dr. Reddy, getting up from his chair. "Give me ten minutes while we prep the therapy room, and I will come and get you." He left the room after saying that.

Archana turned towards me and took my hand. "Are you sure you want to try this Dad?"

I was nervous. Ever since I got Parkinson's, I hadn't been confident or sure of myself. I was not sure how I would do here, but I decided to give it a try nonetheless. "Let's try it once," I said.

After some time, Dr. Reddy came back with a couple of people, and they wheeled me into another room. Archana and Ramani followed behind me.

The other room was bigger and contained a stationary bike. It looked very sophisticated, with lots of wires going from the machine to a big screen as well as a few smaller screens nearby.

"Mr. Niyogi, usually we would ask you to change into something more comfortable to exercise, but since this is only for fifteen minutes, are you okay to continue in the clothes you are wearing?"

I nodded to show that I was okay to proceed.

The people with Dr. Reddy seemed to be his assistants, and they helped me get up and onto the stationary bike. They placed my feet on the pedals and strapped them in. Next, they guided my hands to the handlebars and asked me to hold on tight. Then, they connected a few probes to my chest to monitor my pulse.

"Mr. Niyogi, what is going to happen now is that we will turn on the machine. You don't have to make any effort to pedal if you don't want to; the machine will turn the pedals. You just have to try and relax your muscles and let your legs follow the pedalling motion. We will start very slowly, and we will keep checking in with you. Only if you are comfortable will we increase the speed. Are you okay to start?"

I looked around until I met Archana's and Ramani's eyes. They nodded. I looked at the doctor and gave him a nod.

The doctor went to a computer and pressed a few keys. The pedals started to turn ever so slowly. The seat was very comfortable, but my legs were resisting the motion at first. The doctor stepped closer and told me to relax my legs. This helped me to consciously tell myself to relax, and then it got better. The screen in front of me was showing the number twenty. Dr. Reddy came over again and explained that the number on the screen represented the revolutions per minute.

"For an average cyclist travelling on a flat road, the revolutions per minute is seventy to eighty. We started at twenty for you; if you want to increase the speed, let me know," he said with a gentle hand on my back.

Archana came over to me and asked, "Are you doing okay Dad? Are you good to continue?"

My face must have shown the pain I was feeling, prompting Archana to come and check on me.

"Yes...I am okay..." I said, my breath quickening. After about five minutes, I looked at the doctor and asked him to increase the speed.

The doctor increased the speed to thirty revolutions per minute. "Let me know if this is uncomfortable, Mr. Niyogi."

I stuck to this speed for the rest of the fifteen minutes. Once the timer went off on the screen, the machine automatically started slowing down the pedalling speed, gradually bringing it to a complete stop with the pedals in a horizontal position.

Immediately the doctor's assistants came to unhook me from the machine, removed the probes and unstrapped my feet. The activity left me with a good feeling, although my muscles were in more pain than before.

I found that I had a little more control over my movements, and I was able to dismount almost all by myself. I stretched my hands outward to try and stretch my aching back and did not feel the imbalance that I usually felt when standing fully upright.

I took the few steps to the wheelchair and lowered myself into it with only a little help from the assistants.

I turned towards Archana and Ramani and could see them smiling. *Did they too notice the change that I felt?*

"How do you feel, Mr. Niyogi?" asked Dr. Reddy, coming up next to me.

"I feel a lot of pain in my legs and back, but I feel good," I said.

"That is excellent. I want you to go home today and pay attention to how long you continue to feel good before you start feeling the same as before the session."

I said that I would, and we headed back to the car. On the way home, I laid my head on the headrest to rest, and I watched the trees on the side of the road swish past the car.

There was a bottle of water in the door. I picked it up and took a small sip, and with some effort, I was able to swallow the water. Ramani noticed this and took my free hand in hers. She held it the whole way home.

Chapter 9 - Kiran Singh

I received a message from Archana informing me that they went to the clinic and that they were going to start with therapy sessions for Mr. Niyogi three times a week. Now I had to figure out how to sneak Mr. Niyogi away for at least an hour, either before or after his therapy sessions, so he could start looking at the work and get familiar with what needed to be done.

I had no clue how to make that happen. I approached my cousin Saurabh to tell him about the situation. We were sitting in his office, which had large glass walls overlooking the floor of the dance studio. There was a dance class in progress. He and I could see the group of dancers moving gracefully to the music, led by an instructor. The instructor was an elderly lady, but her body did not move like that of an elderly person. Her movements were graceful and elegant. She moved so well that even some of the younger dancers had trouble keeping up with her.

I told Saurabh about Mr. Niyogi, his health condition and that he wanted to do something by himself to prove to himself that he was not merely surviving with the help of his family on a daily basis. He wanted to prove to himself and others that he could still contribute to society with whatever he had left.

"So you see, for that reason he wants to try his best to attempt working on something that will be useful to many people, and accounting, finance and auditing is what he knows best," I said to Saurabh.

"That is a very brave thing he seems to want to do, Kiran, considering his condition. But why does he not want his family to know? It is going to be hard enough for him to try and do this work without everyone around him supporting him," remarked Saurabh, scratching his head, "let alone doing this without his family knowing about it."

"Well, he does not want his family to find out about this initially because he wants to be sure that he can really do the work and that he is not going to end up charging at windmills like Don Quixote."

"I don't understand why he would be embarrassed to share his attempt with his own family...anyway, it is not my place to have an opinion on that. So, you want to help him and you want my help?"

"Yes, I do," I answered. "Is there any way you can help sneak out Mr. Niyogi from the clinic so I can work with him for an hour or so every time he comes for therapy?"

"Hmm, let me think. How could we do that?" Saurabh turned his attention to the dancers and the instructor, and he was lost in thought for a minute.

"Do you know anyone that works at the clinic?" I prodded.

"I know Anitha Suraj. She is the office admin at the clinic; we are good friends. I will have to involve her and will need help from her to make this happen."

"Okay. Do you think she will help?"

"That I don't know my dear Kiran," said Saurabh casually, not sounding either too optimistic or pessimistic, which was his usual nature.

"Well, can we ask her?"

"Yes, we can ask her," said Saurabh with a sigh. "It's a lot to ask of someone, you know...but I respect what Mr. Niyogi is trying to do. It's not going to be easy for anyone. Let's ask Anitha and see what she says. We may have to take her out for a coffee. We'll get a Hot Velvet coffee for her from CCD."

He then called out to the dance instructor, "Miss Sharmila, I will be right back; my cousin needs some help, okay?" The dance instructor gave him a thumbs-up, and off we went.

We walked over to the Café Coffee Day, which was in the same complex, and picked up a Hot Velvet coffee for Anitha. I paid for the famously delicious coffee and we went over to the clinic with it.

Anitha was in her office talking to someone. We waited outside until she was free, and after her guest left, Saurabh knocked on her glass door. Anitha looked up with a smile and gestured for us to come in and sit down.

We sat down, and Saurabh placed the cup of coffee in front of her ceremoniously. She looked at the cup, smelled the delicious coffee and took it in her hands.

"What do you need Saurabh?" she asked with a smile.

"What do you mean Anitha? I don't need anything. I just came to say hi and bring you this coffee. I know how hard you work. This is my cousin Kiran, by the way...Kiran, Anitha, Anitha, Kiran."

We shook hands and said our nice-to-meet-yous.

Addressing me, Anitha said, "Saurabh never comes by unless he wants something from me, and if he has brought me coffee without even asking me if I wanted one, it means that he needs something really big."

"Hey...that's not true Kiran; don't believe her," he said to me playfully, "I am always this nice to her."

"No honestly, tell me what you want? Or get out, I am busy," said Anitha, still smiling.

"Okay fine. If you really want to help me, I do need something from you. It is a big favour, and I am not even sure if you can pull it off."

Anitha leaned forward and put the coffee cup on the table. She seemed interested to know what Saurabh wanted now that he had framed it as a challenge.

"Let me be the judge of that...go on; tell me what you want?"

"Okay, let me start by saying that I recently referred a new patient to you," said Saurabh, taking full credit for sending Mr. Niyogi over to Anitha's clinic. "Mr. Niyogi, a Parkinson's patient?"

"Hmm, let me see," said Anitha as she turned to her computer to check if they had a patient by that name. "Well, he has been here once for a free sample session, so he is hardly a patient. But go on; what about him?"

"Mr. Niyogi is my cousin's former boss, and he is a very nice man. There is something that he wants to do, and he might need your help to pull it off."

"Well, if he becomes a patient here, we will provide him with the best therapy that we have, and that will help him become more active and gain more control over his movements and mind. Don't worry about that at all; he is in good hands. You don't have to ask that as a favour. He will be treated with the utmost care."

"We have no doubt that he will receive great care at your clinic. What we need from you is a bit beyond that," said Saurabh, using his politest, sincerest tone.

Anitha looked unsure and a bit wary of what Saurabh was going to ask. When it came to the clinic and the clinic's patients, she probably had to be very careful to follow all the safety procedures prescribed by their insurance providers and the Medical Council of India. Any deviation from the standard procedures could harm the patient and also damage the reputation of the clinic.

"What are we talking about here?" asked Anitha. By now she had put the coffee aside and did not care if it was getting cold.

"I will let Kiran explain that," said Saurabh, pointing at me.

My throat went dry for a second, and I had to swallow a couple of times to release the words stuck in my throat.

"Before I ask you what we wanted to ask you, I have to tell you a bit about Mr. Niyogi," I began. "He is an amazing person, a very nice man, such a nice boss and an excellent CA. When he was working at Saran Airlines with me, he had the full trust of management, and there were never any lapses in accounting practices under his watch; he was that good. And he was such a go-getter—"

"I like him already," said Anitha.

I continued, "He retired a few years ago because of back problems, and I kind of lost touch with him. A month ago, I found out that he was suffering from Parkinson's and had become completely dependent on his family to take care of his needs. When I met him, he said that he was so frustrated that he had become like this. He was always the one that others depended on, but now he was dependent on every one just to survive. I am sure you have seen many such people in your work at the clinic here..."

"I have. It is such a sad situation."

"It surely is. Like I was saying, when I met him, he expressed a wish to do something again. Something more than just lying on his bed waiting to be taken care of by others. At that time, I told him about this problem that we are having at the office related to the company finances. That seemed to give him an idea, and he wanted to do his part to try and solve the issue with the finances."

"Hmm, I am sure that the therapy he'll get at our clinic will help him do some of these things."

"Yes, that is what we are hoping for, but there is one problem," I said, pausing to see Anitha's reaction. She continued to stay fully focused on what I was saying.

"His family loves him a lot, I mean a lot, and they are focusing all their energy on taking care of his needs. He is not sure that they will understand his need to work on the project I told you about, and he believes that they will not let him do the work he wants to do at our company."

"I can see why his family might feel that way," said Anitha. "If I were in their position, that is how I would have felt too. I would not want him to exert himself unnecessarily and would want him to focus on getting better."

"In addition to his family possibly not allowing him to do what he wants, he is also a little unsure that he can do the work, given his health condition," I explained. "He wants to try and do some work first; see if he can add value. Then he'd be able to go to his family and show them that he can do the work and that they should support him."

"I have seen people suffering from Parkinson's losing all motivation in life. They can hardly function on a day-to-day basis, let alone dare to do something like this. It is admirable what Mr. Niyogi wants to do."

"You are exactly right, and that is why I too am doing everything I can to help him with this endeavour of his."

Anitha took a deep breath. She took a few sips from the coffee cup, then put the cup aside again and crossed her arms. She looked directly at me and said, "Okay, I see why you want to help him; it is a noble cause. I am not against helping him. But it is a matter of IF I can help him, and that depends on what you are going to ask of me."

She then waited for Saurabh or me to speak.

"This is what I want to ask," I began. "Whenever Mr. Niyogi comes here for a therapy session, can you tell his family that he needs to rest for a while after the session? And while his family thinks he is resting, could you either allow me into the room so I can work with him or help us sneak him out the back door into Saurabh's dance studio? If we could get an hour that would be great. "

"A lot of what you're asking for goes against our care procedures and policies, and I can't risk the reputation of my clinic to facilitate something that the family of the patient has not agreed to. I am sorry, but I cannot help you," Anitha said.

Saurabh and I sat back in our chairs, looking dejected. Saurabh spoke first. "I understand your position Anitha. It is one thing helping a friend out in your personal time and a whole other thing helping a friend out using your employer's resources and facilities. Do you have any ideas on how this can be done without compromising your position at the clinic?"

Anitha once again paused to take a few sips of her coffee. She looked at the clock on the wall behind me and Saurabh, probably thinking that she had to get back to work. All three of us sat there in silence for a couple of minutes.

"Give me a minute; I need to go to the washroom," said Anitha, leaving us in the room as she stepped out.

She came back five minutes later and closed the door to her office behind her. "I think I have an idea. We offer a pick-up and drop-off service for our patients with limited mobility, in our patient transportation van. I can offer that to Mr. Niyogi and his family when they come to register him as a patient. We can then figure out a spot for the driver to stop, and maybe you can get into the van and work with Mr. Niyogi on the way here and on the way back? Would that work?"

"That could work..." I said, pausing for a second to think it through. I would have to work this out with my team at the office so I could be here three times a week while being covered at work. I figured I'd be able to make it happen. *Yes, this can work. I will make it work.*

"Okay super," said Saurabh, "problem solved. Anitha, as always, you are an amazing lady. You always find a way. Thank you so much."

"Yes, thank you so much Anitha; I really appreciate it," I said.

"You are welcome, although you have to do what you can to convince your Mr. Niyogi and his family to take the transportation provided by the clinic, which is not free by the way."

"Got it," I said. "I will do my best to encourage them to take the transportation."

Saurabh and I left Anitha's office, and I thanked Saurabh again for his help in this matter. I now had to find a way to convince Archana.

Later that evening, I called Archana.

"Hi Archana, how are you?" I said.

"Hi Mr. Singh! I am doing well; how are you?"

"Please call me Kiran. You don't have to be so formal with me."

"Ha ha, okay, Kiran. We went to the clinic, and my dad liked the demo session he got; we are planning to sign him up for a few sessions at the clinic."

"Oh, that is good to know. I am sure it will help Mr. Niyogi a lot. I have heard so many good things from my relative about how the sessions helped him. My cousin also said they used the transportation provided by the clinic. They have a special purpose-built van for patients; almost like a mini ambulance. Apparently it's very comfortable. Mr. Niyogi will be able to travel lying down if it is more comfortable for him that way."

"Oh okay. Thanks for letting me know about the transportation. I think we will take it; my dad's back pains a lot whenever he has to sit down for a long time."

"You are most welcome. When are you planning to start the sessions?"

"As soon as possible; maybe from Monday."

"Great, great...well, I am sure this will benefit Mr. Niyogi in more ways than one. Take care Archana; please let me know if I can be of any assistance."

"Will do, thank you Kiran. Good evening."

Chapter 10 - Mr. Niyogi

Archana signed me up at the clinic for therapy. She told me that the clinic offered transportation in their purpose-built van from the apartment to the clinic and back.

"I have seen the van Dad," she was saying, "it has a specially design seat that can fully recline if need be, and you can travel in complete comfort. It only transports one patient at a time, and there will be a nurse in the back with you who will ensure that you are comfortable throughout the ride. It also has bathroom facilities, so if there is a lot of traffic and you need to pee or something, they will help you right there. I think we should sign up for the transportation as well. Mom and I will drive to the clinic in my car, so we'll be there if you need anything. What do you say?"

"You or Ramani can't travel in the van with me? Will the nurse be able to help me with everything? What if I need to poop urgently?"

"I asked about that, and the administrator at the clinic, a lady named Anitha Suraj, said that the nurse will be able to help with anything. It will be a male nurse."

"Okay," I said.

Although I had signed up with the clinic, I had not heard from Kiran about how this was going to help me work on the audit. *Will he come to the clinic? How will I be able to work if Archana and Ramani are also going to be at the clinic?*

I was glad that they were coming to the clinic with me, but I wondered how I'd be able to work if they were there too. I made a mental note of the things I had to take with me, like my glasses and a pen.

A pen? It had been two years since I had written anything with my own hand. Since my Parkinson's had progressed, I had not been able to hold a pen steady enough to write. But if I had to write, I was going to find a way somehow.

While I was lost in my thoughts, Archana had spoken with the clinic to make the arrangements.

"Your first therapy session is tomorrow," said Archana, interrupting my thoughts and bringing my attention back to her. "It is at 5 p.m., and the van will be here at 3:30 p.m. I won't be here then, so Mom and Manoj will help you into the van. I will come at 4:30 and bring Mom to the clinic with me."

"Okay my dear," I said. The thought of going alone, without Ramani or Archana by my side, caused a sudden pang of anxiety and I felt like I had to pee. "Can you ask Manoj to come help me? I need to pee."

Archana left the room, and Manoj arrived to help me to the washroom.

At around 2 p.m. the next day, Ramani and Manoj fed me through the feeding tube so I would have enough food in me to last until I was back from the clinic. I was to leave at 3:30 p.m., spend an hour at the clinic, leave at 6 p.m. and be back home by 7:30 p.m. at the latest.

"I have already prepared your liquid meals so that everything is ready and you can have a meal as soon as you are back my dear, is that okay?" Ramani asked. "If you need to, you can have water while at the clinic."

I nodded to convey that I understood. Then Manoj helped me dress in comfortable tracksuit pants and a cotton shirt. He also put socks on my feet before sliding them into my slip-on walking shoes. By the time all of this was done, Ramani got a call on her phone, and she came to tell me that the van was downstairs.

I got into the wheelchair, and Manoj and Ramani took me down the elevator to the clinic's waiting van.

As I approached the van, the side door slid open, and I could see a complicated-looking seat inside. The driver opened his door and got out of the van, while a male nurse stepped out on the passenger side. The driver pressed a button just inside the open door, which made the seat inside the van slide out and down. With help from Manoj and Ramani, I got up from my wheelchair and sat down in the van. The nurse clipped my seat belt in place and stepped back. He also gestured for the others to step back, and then the driver pressed another button. This time, the seat slowly slid back into its position inside the van with me sitting on it.

The van was indeed fancy, and getting in with the automatic sliding seat was very convenient and comfortable. I looked around in the van. There was an empty seat next to me and an open area behind me with many shelves on each side. There was also a seat behind the seat next to me. I looked at Ramani, nervous to be going out alone with two strangers. *What if they can't hear me calling them because my voice cannot reach them? How will I ask for help?*

I was sure I did not ask this question out loud, but the nurse came to my side and said, "Mr. Niyogi, this red button near you is for you to call us. I will be sitting behind you there, and I will be able to help you with anything that you may need while en route to the clinic."

I nodded with a weak smile, which was all I could muster. I was nervous, and I hoped it did not show too much.

The driver got into the van, the nurse got in behind me and the sliding door closed automatically. I waved to Ramani, and off we went. The van drove for about a kilometer or so and then stopped in front of a small shopping complex. The door on the other side opened, and I was surprised to see Kiran standing outside the van with a pile of documents.

Aha, so Kiran is going to come with me to the clinic?

"Hello Mr. Niyogi, how are you?" asked Kiran as he got into the van.

As Kiran got in, the nurse stepped out of the van. "Sir, I was told that Mr. Singh needs to talk to you about something important," said the nurse. "So, I will be sitting in the front with the driver. You can press the red button if you need me for anything."

I thanked the nurse, who closed the door and got in the front of the van next to the driver.

"I am okay, thank you," I told Kiran. "How are you?"

"I am doing okay sir. I am glad you opted for the clinic's transportation. This was the only way we could spend some time together to work on the audit. I will come with you on the way to the clinic and on the way back too, so we should get around two hours of work done every time you go to the clinic. Is that okay?"

"Okay," I said. A hundred negative thoughts were running through my head, each one more discouraging than the next.

"Let's get right into it, sir. I have with me some statements. Do you want to go through them and let me know how you want to tackle this?"

"Okay, let's try that," I said. I took out my glasses while Kiran looked for and turned on a light right above me, which lit up the documents in my hands. I tried to read them. The letters were all dancing in front of my eyes, and I couldn't focus. The constantly moving van did not make things easier.

"I cannot...read...clearly," I said, feeling ashamed of myself. *How can I be of any help if I can't even read a statement?*

"Okay, let's try this," said Kiran. He took the statements from me and started reading them out loud. I closed my eyes and listened intently. This seemed better.

"Can you read the items one by one, slowly, and pause for a few seconds in between each item so I can think about them a little?" I asked.

Kiran started reading the items out more slowly and clearly. Each item on the statement had a date, a description, a credit account name, a debit account name, the amount and the name of the person who initiated the transaction.

There were five statements, each with fifty to sixty items. Kiran read them out to me, and I listened closely to determine if, based on my past experience, any of the transactions seemed odd, either inflated or deflated. There were a few transactions that seemed a little off, but that could have been because the business had grown since I left the job. It was a much bigger organization now. I asked Kiran to pause and re-read those items.

As many times as he re-read them, I could not think of why they seemed off to me. I decided to let him continue with the list and the rest of the statements. We had gone through four out of the five statements, and I did not have anything useful to share with Kiran. Nothing useful to contribute. I was wasting his time. *Is this how it is going to be for the duration of this audit? Could it be that these statements are all good, and that some other statements we have yet to look at will hold some clues to tell us where the money went missing? Or could it be that I am simply not of much use?*

Kiran had just started reading the fifth statement when we arrived at the clinic. He told me that we would continue on the way back.

"Okay Kiran...I am sorry I could not figure out what was wrong with these statements," I said guiltily.

"Don't worry sir. Maybe there was nothing wrong with these. I've also gone over these statements and found nothing wrong with them. Anyway, it's time for your therapy. I will join you on the way back, and we will go over some more statements then."

Kiran opened the door on his side, got out and closed the door behind him.

The door on my side slid open, and the nurse was there with a wheelchair. The automatic seat slowly started moving out of the vehicle so I could get up and move into the wheelchair.

Ramani and Archana were waiting in the lounge of the clinic and came up to me as soon as they saw me. "How was the ride Dad? Was it comfortable? No problems?" Archana asked a few rapid-fire questions.

I told her that everything was okay and that the ride had been comfortable.

Archana then went to reception to tell them that I was there for my therapy, and they asked us to wait for a few minutes. After five to ten minutes, a couple of technicians came out to the lounge and took me into a therapy room. Archana and Ramani followed us.

Once inside the room, the staff asked Archana and Ramani to wait in an adjoining room with a large glass window that looked into the therapy room.

Dr. Surendra Reddy came into the room and said, "How are you Mr. Niyogi? Today will be your first therapy session. We have divided the session into two parts; one part is the same as you did on the day you were here previously. The second part of the session will be the electrical impulse treatment. We will do a very low-intensity treatment today just for five minutes to see how you respond, and later on we will adjust it based on your response. Is that okay? Shall we get started?"

"Yes, let's start," I said, both looking forward to it and dreading the pain that I knew was coming.

Dr. Reddy's staff gently helped me onto the stationary bike, strapped me in and stepped back before turning on the machine. The pedals turned very slowly at first, and gradually the speed increased to a speed of twenty-five revolutions per minute, which was far from the seventy to eighty that a healthy cyclist would be pushing for. But for me, it was almost on the edge of my capacity to pedal. I started sweating and taking deep breaths.

Dr. Reddy came to my side and said, "Initially you may feel yourself getting out of breath, but please do keep going, and you should settle into a rhythm soon."

After about twenty-five minutes of constant pedalling, I was really tired and was panting with effort. At Dr. Reddy's instruction, the two technicians came to help me get off the bike. The pedals came to a stop, and the technicians unhooked me from the all the sensors and unstrapped me from the bike. They then helped me into the wheelchair nearby. I was sweating and tired, and I was thirsty as heck.

I made a gesture with my thumb to indicate that I wanted water. A cup of water was brought to me, and I took a few sips. Magically and thankfully my throat cooperated and helped me swallow the water. It took me ten minutes, but I finished all the water in the glass.

Dr. Reddy came to check my pulse and asked me how I was doing.

"I am doing...well. Everything hurts, but I feel good," I said. I turned to Archana and Ramani, whose eyes were fully focused on me. "I am fine!" I said a little more loudly. I was not sure whether they heard it, but they both nodded happily and waved at me. I waved back.

"Now, Mr. Niyogi, we will proceed with the second therapy session, the electrical impulse therapy. Is that okay?"

I swallowed once and said, "Okay, let's try that, but I can't sit up for too long now; I need to lie down."

"Yes, you will be lying down during this treatment," said Dr Reddy.

They wheeled me to the next room, which had a similar adjoining viewing area where Ramani and Archana could sit and watch me.

I was helped to sit on a bed, and a technician took my shirt off. I could feel someone put a gel-like substance on a few spots along my spine. A few cold metal pieces then touched my spine where the gel was applied. They then pulled my shirt down and carefully arranged the wires to one side before asking me to lie down on my back.

Dr. Reddy was at my side once again and said, "Mr. Niyogi, we have attached a few impulse connectors to your back. We will keep monitoring you, and we will start the impulses in a sequence starting from the lowest point on your spine all the way up to the one right below your neck. You may or may not feel the impulses immediately. It may take some time for you to register them because we are going to start with 0.5 volts and slowly go all the way up to 1.5 volts. Are you ready?"

I shrugged and said, "Yes, I am ready." *I am ready to try anything doctor.*

For the first ten minutes, I could not feel anything. And then, slowly, I started to feel the tiniest of pin pricks along my spine. After another ten minutes, I could feel the pricks much more clearly. They were going off in a sequence: beep, beep, beep, beep...just like decorative string lights. I imagined that my spine was glowing with each pin prick.

I did not feel any different, but once the impulses stopped, my mind kept expecting the pin pricks to continue.

I slowly got up and stood holding the bed. The technicians rushed over to help me get into the wheelchair. I thanked the doctor and the technicians, and they wheeled me back to the reception area. Ramani and Archana were waiting for me. They were beaming; I did not know why. I smiled back and said that I would see them back home.

The van was waiting in front of the clinic, the door open and the automatic seat already ready for me. Archana and Ramani waited until I was seated, strapped in and the door closed, and then they started towards Archana's car.

Once the van started to move, I turned to see Kiran sitting in the back chair. He then moved to sit beside me.

"How was the session sir? Was it okay?"

"It was okay Kiran; it felt good. I feel full of energy somehow, even though I pedalled for so long on the bike."

"That is good sir! Are you okay to look at the statements or do you want to rest?"

"I am good to go through the statements. Let's do it," I said. "Can you read the statements out to me once more?"

"Yes of course sir." And then Kiran started going through the first statement again, item by item.

After the therapy session, I found myself more alert, and even though my leg muscles and back were in pain, I was able to pay closer attention to the words coming out of Kiran's mouth.

"Item number twenty-four: 23 October 2020, Laundry charges for seat covers – Mumbai hospitality branch, credit account – Mumbai ticket sales, debit account – hospitality maintenance expenses, ₹56,897.75."

Something was not right about this transaction. It was not right for hospitality expenses to be directly funded by ticket sales. Ticket sales were to be debited to ticket sales income, and from that account, money was to be debited into the hospitality expenses account. From there, it was supposed to be disbursed to individual maintenance expenses.

"Can you mark this transaction for us to double-check Kiran? Individual expenses should not have been credited to ticket sales directly," I said. I sounded more confident than I had felt or sounded on the way to the clinic. "Who entered this transaction?"

"It was done by the Mumbai accounts payable department."

"Is that new? Before I retired, expense transactions were entered by the hospitality department manager. Can you find out who from the accounting department entered these?"

"Sure sir. I will make a note and check on that."

Kiran then continued reading the statements out to me. There were sixteen other transactions that ended with 97.75, all originating from various departments of the Mumbai office. The Mumbai branch was the biggest of the branches and had more than twelve thousand employees back when I worked at Saran. The global pandemic led to drastic reductions in flights, and the total number of transactions recorded were also down drastically, corresponding to the reduced flights. In spite of that, the laundry expenses that were recorded seemed much lower than what I would have expected them to be.

Another anomaly that stood out to me was the number of transactions that ended with 97.75. Was it because someone wanted to easily identify the fictitious transactions they had entered into the system? Or had they been going so quickly that they did not have time to think up a whole assortment of fake numbers?

I asked Kiran to check them nonetheless. Kiran continued to read all the statements out to me, and I was able to flag twenty-three more transactions that I wanted him to look into.

The van turned into the shopping complex where Kiran had gotten in earlier. He thanked me and quickly got out as we said our goodbyes. The door closed, and the van drove away towards our apartment complex. Ramani and Manoj were waiting for me by the time the van pulled up to the curb.

The door slid open, and my seat started humming as it slid out of the van and lowered until my feet touched the ground. I pushed up and stood up all by myself. I told Ramani that I would walk to the elevator, and I thanked the van driver and the nurse before they drove off.

The distance from the van to the elevator was around twenty meters. I was slow, but I felt that my movements were more controlled. I had more control over my legs than I had experienced in many months.

Ramani was holding my left hand and Manoj my right. We made it to the elevator and then from the elevator to my room, where Manoj quickly took off my shoes and ran to bring me my food.

"You sipped a whole glass of water at the clinic by yourself. I was so happy to see that," said Ramani. "Do you want to try to sip some soup by yourself, without the tube?"

My improved walking ability had given me some extra confidence, and I said, "Okay, let's try."

Ramani took the bowl from Manoj and brought a bit of soup to my mouth using a spoon. I pulled the liquid into my mouth. The soup turned out to be much thicker than the water I had sipped and was much harder to swallow. I shook my head at the next spoonful and said, "I am too tired. I can't swallow."

Ramani smiled with understanding and asked Manoj to inject the soup through the feeding tube. After ingesting the bowl of soup, I could feel the warmth spreading through my stomach. My eyelids were drooping, and I asked to use the bathroom. Manoj brought the urine collector to the bed, and I relieved myself into it.

With help from Ramani, I lay down on the bed, and within a few minutes I was in a deep sleep.

Chapter 11 - Kiran Singh

After working with Mr. Niyogi on the first day of his therapy sessions, I went to the office and started to investigate the transactions Mr. Niyogi had identified. At first, I could not find out much about them. I then started looking into who had entered the transactions to see if I could talk to that person. The transactions were marked with the initials "GM."

I called up the Mumbai office to find out who "GM" was.

"Hello, this is Kiran Singh from the head office in Bangalore," I began. "We are doing an accounts audit and had some questions about a few transactions. Are you able to help me out?"

On the other end of the line was Supriya Kamble, the head of accounts for the Mumbai office. "Yes, of course. How can I help?" she asked.

"On some of the transactions, I see the initials 'GM' as the user who recorded the transactions. Do you know who GM is?"

"Hmm, let me see here." I could hear typing sounds on a computer keyboard as I waited. "There are two people with the initials GM. Govardhan Mankar and Mihir Gokhale. Mihir Gokhale always enters his initials as GM, even though it would seem that his initials should be MG. Is everything okay? Was there a problem with any of the transactions entered by these two people?"

"We are still looking into them," I said, not wanting to raise any false alarms without knowing for sure that there was some wrongdoing. "I will let you know as soon as I find something. Can you please give me the contact numbers for both these people?"

"I will send you Mihir's contact details, but Govardhan is no longer employed by the company. He quit his job a month back. He said that he inherited some money from his grandfather and that he was going back to his village to buy a farm."

Interesting. Inherited money from his grandfather around the time the money went missing from the company?

"Oh okay, thank you. I will contact Mihir to find out more."

I cut the call with Supriya and dialed Mihir's number. The phone rang six times before it was picked up.

"Hello, Mihir here."

"Hi Mihir, this is Kiran Singh from the head office, accounts department. I wanted to reach out to you about some transactions you entered. Can you help me understand them?"

"Yes...of course sir. Please let me know how I can help."

Was that hesitation I heard in his voice?

I then questioned Mihir about each of the transactions recorded by this "GM," including those identified by Mr. Niyogi. I asked him for more details and any supporting documents that were related to each transaction.

Mihir was able to give me the full details for almost all of the transactions he recorded, including one from the suspicious list of transactions. But he had no information about thirty-eight out of the thirty-nine suspicious transactions. The one transaction that he had information on did end with 97.75, and that involved a vendor known to the hospitality department.

When I pressed him for information about the remaining thirty-eight, he said that he did not make those transactions. The one he did make was because he was asked to cover for Govardhan one day when Govardhan called in sick.

I then asked if he had any information on his system about the vendors involved in the thirty-eight transactions. Mihir looked and found that the vendor was a company called Julia Cleaning Services, based out of Nasik, Maharashtra. Mihir said that it was a C vendor, only used rarely when the primary A vendor and secondary B vendors were not available.

I asked for more information about Julia Cleaning Services and whether Mihir could contact the company to find out if they had received the payments that were recorded as made to them.

Thirty minutes later my phone rang. "Hello, Kiran speaking."

It was Mihir. "Hi Mr. Singh. I contacted Julia Cleaning Services, and I unfortunately have some bad news. Our contact at Julia Cleaning Services confirmed that they only invoiced us once during that period and not the other times. They only received the one payment that I recorded and never received any other payments."

"Okay, thank you Mihir. Can you please inform Supriya about this? This is serious."

"Will do, Mr. Singh," said Mihir, and he cut the call.

I tallied up all the transactions where Julia Cleaning Services was the recipient. Not including the one transaction Mihir had entered, the total came to ₹9,983,793.25. *Wow, almost ₹1 million. I have to let Mr. Saran know about this right away.*

I double-checked my numbers and printed the transactions out on a sheet of paper. Then I headed to Mr. Saran's office and asked his secretary if I could see him, telling her that it was urgent. She said that he was having his lunch, but I insisted, so she called Mr. Saran anyway. He asked her to send me in.

"This had better be important Kiran. You know I don't like to be disturbed when I am eating," said Mr. Saran once I closed the door behind me.

"Sir, I did some work with Mr. Niyogi yesterday, and we went over five to six statements for the month of October 2020."

"And so?"

"Mr. Niyogi identified around thirty-eight transactions that he asked me to verify. It turned out that thirty-seven of those transactions were fraudulent. The total amount comes to almost ₹1 million. I think the money was stolen by a former employee of the Mumbai office, Govardhan Mankar. He recorded transactions as payments made to Julia Cleaning Services, but the company never received that money. There are no invoices from them for those transactions, yet money was withdrawn from the company bank account via cheques issued to Julia Cleaning Services."

"How did we not catch this earlier?" Mr. Saran was on his feet, his lunch forgotten. "How was the payment issued without someone verifying the invoices?"

"I don't know that yet sir. I am going to find out more about this. Supriya has been informed."

Mr. Saran picked up his phone. "Get Supriya Kamble on the phone," he said to his secretary. As the call got connected, he said that I could go, and so I left.

I was sweating profusely. I could hear Mr. Saran yelling at Supriya as I walked away from his office.

On the one hand, I was scared about what was going to happen to me for missing this substantial fraud. On the other hand, I was happy that Mr. Niyogi had caught it. He would be very happy to hear that neither retirement nor Parkinson's had dulled his sharp mind.

A couple of hours later, I got a call from Mr. Saran. "Niyogi was always amazing at catching such things," he said. "I am glad he is helping us. I want you to ask him for more help. See if you can go back six months and find out if there were more suspicious transactions. And more importantly, ask if Niyogi can teach you to identify such fraud too."

"Yes Mr. Saran. I will ask Mr. Niyogi to teach me how to detect this kind of fraud."

"And do what you have to do to make him comfortable while he is helping us."

"Yes sir, will do," I said.

I spent the rest of the day filling in the paperwork required to account for this loss. I then shared the information with the company lawyers so they could initiate the appropriate action against Govardhan Mankar and whomever else had helped him get away with it.

Mr. Niyogi's next therapy session was arranged for two days later. I printed out the statements from September that I wanted to review with him.

On the day of the therapy session, I drove to the shopping complex where the van would stop to pick me up. I parked my vehicle and waited in the same the spot where the van had picked me up last time. I was early, so I had to wait fifteen minutes before the van showed up.

The van stopped in front of me, the nurse got out of the seat next to Mr. Niyogi and moved to the front passenger seat.

"Hello Mr. Niyogi! How are you doing?" I asked as I got into the seat next to him, closed the door and put on my seat belt.

"I am doing okay Kiran, how are you?"

"I am doing well sir. Did you have any problems because of the last therapy session? Was everything okay?"

"It was okay until last night. I was able to walk around at home for a few days after the therapy session, but this morning it became difficult to walk again," he said, shaking his head and looking down as he wrung his hands.

"Well, I hope today's session will help you sir," I said, trying to sound positive.

"You always were the optimistic type, Kiran," said Mr. Niyogi. "Tell me, did the transactions that we looked at last time help in any way? Did you find out more about them?"

"Oh yes sir! I have been waiting to tell you this good news," I said, rubbing my hands together. "We were able to trace those transactions to an ex-employee of the Mumbai office. We think he stole almost ₹1 million just during the month of October, all from thirty-seven out of the thirty-eight transactions you identified."

"Oh, that is good news. I am happy that I was of some help!" said Mr. Niyogi, a smile spreading across his face.

"Yes sir, that was very good. Mr. Saran was furious that we did not catch it earlier though, and Supriya from the Mumbai office got an earful from him. I think now she is busy trying to find a way to get the money back."

"Hmm. I hope you all find a way to get the money back soon," said Mr. Niyogi.

"Yes sir, the lawyers have been engaged. They are working on trying to locate the person. Anyway, today I brought all the statements from September. Mr. Saran wanted us to look at the past six months' statements to try and find more such instances of fraud. He wants all of this to be discovered before the company gets listed on the stock exchange. Saran Airlines is going to offer an IPO soon."

"Okay, let's go over the statements then."

"Oh sir," I said, lowering my voice and moving a bit closer to Mr. Niyogi, "I hope you will keep the IPO news to yourself. Not many people know this."

"Who am I going to tell Kiran?" said Mr. Niyogi. "Don't worry."

"Thank you, sir. And since we found out about Govardhan, the Mumbai office has gone and looked into all of his older transactions. They found that, over the last six months, he entered forty-five such transactions, amounting to a total of ₹2.6 million. And this discovery is all thanks to you sir!" I said to Mr. Niyogi, who beamed with joy when he heard that.

"That is good to know Kiran," he said, "let's go over these statements to see if we can identify more."

"Yes sir," I said, and then I started reading out the transactions one by one. We went through three statements, and Mr. Niyogi seemed unsure about ten transactions. He asked me to mark around seven of them.

When the van reached the clinic, I got out quickly and said that I would see him after the session. I then went to Saurabh's dance studio to see if I could sit there while I waited for Mr. Niyogi to finish his session. There was a dance class going on, so I went into Saurabh's office and sat down to go over the transactions myself to see if I could identify anything that I could ask Mr. Niyogi's opinion about.

About an hour later, I went back to the same spot as before and waited for the van to come pick me up. Fifteen minutes after the hour, the van pulled up near me and I got in. Mr. Niyogi arrived soon after that. Just like last time, he seemed to be in a much better mood after the session. He also seemed much more alert than he had been earlier.

As soon as he saw me, he beckoned for me to come closer and patted the seat next to him. He sat up a little straighter and leaned forward; he seemed eager to get started.

Mr. Niyogi patiently listened as I read out more statements, and he identified forty-six more transactions for me to follow up on.

We had wrapped up a bit earlier today, and I asked him, "Sir, can you teach me how to identify such cases of fraud? It will help me a lot."

"Yes, of course Kiran, I would be happy to," he said, taking a deep breath and turning to look out the window. He then started counting on his fingers but did not say anything yet.

I got my notebook out so I could capture what he was going to tell me.

"The first thing that I look for is patterns in the transactions. When people are entering real numbers, they may not always follow a pattern, unless it is a fixed retainer type of transaction. Only when entering fake transactions do people automatically start entering the numbers in a more or less repeatable pattern, so you have to watch out for that."

"Like the 97.75 in Govardhan's case?"

"Yes, exactly," said Mr. Niyogi. He continued, "Another thing to watch out for is transaction dates closer to the end of the month. People are always in need of extra cash around that time, or sales folks are looking to make quotas. This is also the case with transactions recorded closer to the end of the workday—people take more risks then and think that nobody is watching.

"The next thing I do is compare the entries with past entries. Do the amounts seem consistent or within 5 to 10% variance compared to the previous years? Although I have not seen the last few years' statements, I did an extrapolation considering inflation, and some of the transactions that I identified stood out. So, you need to watch out for that."

"Hmm, interesting."

"Another thing that is also helpful in identifying fraud is looking at the spending appetite that Saran Airlines usually has for the various services it buys. Since I worked with Mr. Saran for a long time, I know that he usually does not want to spend more than a certain percentage of the total ticket sales for a month on the various expenses. He usually delays payment or asks for a better price from the vendors when his spending limits are being reached or crossed. So, you should watch out for that too."

"Got it. I will make a note of that."

"I will have to rack my brain to think if there are more such rules or criteria that can be used to weed out fraud. I will tell you as they come to me. Actually, let's look at the transactions that I identified today, and I will tell you which ones fall under which type of detection method. "

We went through the forty-six transactions again, and Mr. Niyogi clearly separated them into three to four buckets of fraud-detection types. I made notes on all of those transactions so I would remember the buckets later when I was following up on them.

"Sir, this is amazing, I am so glad that I am getting to learn all of this from you; thank you so much," I said.

"No Kiran, thank you for indulging an old man like me and helping me do something other than lying around on my bed waiting for something to happen." He put his hand over mine and gave it a light squeeze.

The van stopped, and I realized that the one hour it took for the van to make the trip had passed in no time. I thanked Mr. Niyogi and got out of the van. Then I thanked the nurse and the driver and watched the van pull away to drop Mr. Niyogi off at his apartment.

There was a lot more work to be done, and I realized that Saran Airlines would have to find a way to compensate Mr. Niyogi for his work in helping us identify these major gaps in our accounting practices.

Chapter 12 - Mr. Niyogi

anoj brought my wheelchair to the balcony and moved it close to the railing. If I leaned forward, I could see the people walking on the ground. There were people in groups, and there were people walking by themselves. There were couples walking together. The sun was throwing long shadows on the ground. I could see kids playing on the basketball court and people splashing around in the pool beyond.

When we moved into this apartment, Ramani and I used to go walking together. We would take a few laps around the building, the sun in our faces going one way and on our backs the other way.

Ramani used to get in more laps than me, as my Parkinson's kept getting the better of me. The number of laps I could do slowly decreased as I grew sicker, and some days all I could manage was one or even half a lap. I would find a place to sit while Ramani continued her walking. Slowly but surely, my ability to walk kept diminishing, and I became bound to the wheelchair. If the wheelchair did not move, I could not move.

I missed walking with Ramani.

"Mr. Niyogi."

I heard someone call me, and I turned my heard to see who it was. There was no one. Ramani was taking a nap on the sofa in the living room. She usually stayed up in the afternoons watching TV, but today she had been walking slower than usual, holding on to the furniture and walls as she walked. Manoj was probably in the bedroom. My daughter was at work.

"Mr. Niyogi!"

The voice rang out a little louder this time. I looked down at the walking path below the balcony, trying to see if someone was calling me from down there. But no one was looking up or trying to get my attention.

"Mr. Niyogi, please don't ignore me."

I didn't want to admit it, but I knew who it was. It was probably Archana's friend's young son. The friend had been keeping Archana updated on the situation. The friend had not been able to secure the return of her son. With no one helping her, she was suffering at home while her son suffered on a faraway remote island, waiting for a rescue that was not coming. Had he given up hope?

"Mr. Niyogi, you are ignoring me. I beg of you; please don't ignore me."

I put my hand on the railing and laid my head on my arm.

"I am not ignoring you," I whispered into my arm. I did not want anyone to see me responding. "Why do you keep bothering me? What do you want?"

"I want to come home, Mr. Niyogi. I know that you can help me," said the voice shakily.

"I am trying, but I can't make any promises," I continued, keeping my voice down. "I don't have the resources to bring you home, but I am working on finding a way."

"Please....quickly....there is nothing to eat here; we are getting more hopeless by the day."

"I can't give you hope when I have none to give. I am trying, so stop bothering me. You will get home when you get home. Just....stay alive until then. Just stay alive…"

"Mr. Niyogi…." The voice faded away when I heard Ramani walking up to me.

"My dear, did you want something? Were you calling me?"

"No, Ramani, I was just sitting here watching the people walk by."

"Okay; well let's go. I will give you some coffee," said Ramani, unlocking the wheels on my chair and pushing it back into the house. I was glad that she was taking me inside and that I was awake. I did not hear that boy calling me when she was next to me.

Ramani then brought me coffee and injected it into my feeding tube. I wanted so badly to taste the coffee, but because of the tube, the only way I felt it was after it reached my stomach. As the coffee made it to my stomach, I could feel the tiny surge in energy that coffee always brought me.

Ramani sat down next to me with her own cup of coffee. I reached out to hold her hand and said, "Ramani, you are looking very tired today; are you okay?"

"I am okay my dear. It's just that my knees are paining more than usual today; that's all."

"I never thought that I would become like this Ramani. I always thought I would be the one taking care of you," I said.

"Don't think like that my dear. No one asked for this to happen; it just happened. It's out of our hands."

"I don't know if I will ever get better."

"You will get better; stop being so pessimistic," she said, touching my cheek.

"Hmm. I have come to depend on you and Archana and Manoj for everything, I can't even go to the bathroom by myself. I can't even take a bath by myself. And this wretched feeding tube—"

"Look my dear; don't worry about those things. It is all temporary; a passing phase. Trust me. You will get better and you will be doing all those things by yourself in no time. You just keep going to those therapy sessions, and I am sure they will help improve your strength."

"Riding on that bike is so hard; so painful."

"Hmm. But I've seen that you are alert and active for two days after each session. And you have only done ten such sessions so far. You have to keep going. I'm sure you've noticed that you are able to talk for longer and sit up for longer after the therapy. And how many days has it been since you've sat on the balcony? Wasn't it nice to come and sit here and watch what is happening around you?"

"It is nice to sit on the balcony. I like it."

Ramani's favourite soap opera was on TV, with the volume very low.

"Do you know what happened to that boy?" I asked her after sitting in silence for a while.

"Who? Which boy?"

"You know, the son of Archana's friend. I forgot her name."

"Rajamouli? Gopika's son?"

"Ah, yes, him. Is he back home?"

"No, he has not returned yet. Poor boy; stuck on that island in these times when there are so many travel restrictions. I don't know when he will get back home."

"Is someone doing something to bring those people home?" Since it was difficult for me to use my phone these days, I had no way to look up the news or do any research online. The only way I could find out anything was by asking Ramani or Archana to look stuff up for me.

"No, I don't think so. All the government agencies are busy dealing with COVID and its aftermath. They think the people stuck on the island have enough food to survive there until some resources become available. I don't know when that will be."

"Maybe some private companies should do something. Maybe a travel company can send one of their unused ships. I am sure cruises are still not allowed."

"Yeah, maybe your former employer can do something. I'm sure they offer luxury cruises in addition to flights, no?"

"I am not sure; can you go to their website and see?"

"Ah, I don't know how to search properly. Let's wait for Archana; she can find out for you."

"Okay, let's wait for Archana," I said. I continued to sit there with Ramani watching TV, but my mind was elsewhere. *How am I going to ask Mr. Saran to send a ship to an island? Will he even agree? What will happen to Rajamouli if Saran does not agree to send a ship?*

* * *

Later that evening, Archana came into to my room.

"Hi Dad! How are you? Are you feeling better?"

"I am okay my dear."

"Did you eat yet?"

"Yes, I did. How was work today?"

"Oh, you know. Same old; nothing special."

"Archana, can you do something for me? Can you go to the website of Saran Airlines and see if they offer cruises or some other form of sea travel?"

"Why? Are you planning to take a trip somewhere?" Archana asked with a chuckle.

"Just do it; use your phone."

Archana opened up her phone and did a search. Then she started reading out what she found.

"This is what I see on their website: 'Due to the travel restrictions imposed in response to the novel corona virus, the following services are temporarily suspended: Ferry services between the cities of Chennai and

Port Blair, passenger boat services between Cochin and Lakshadweep, luxury cruises from Mumbai and Mangaluru ports to the Maldives, passenger boat services from Nagapattinam to Kankesanthurai, Jaffna, Sri Lanka and all other services.

"In anticipation of the travel restrictions being lifted in the future, we are adding many new sea-travel options and services. Saran Airlines has been working to acquire state-of-the-art passenger ships to support the travel needs of its customers.'

"Looks like they do offer passenger travel options by sea, Dad. Why did you want to know?"

"Your mom and I were talking about your friend's son, Rajamouli, and how nice it would be if some transport company can offer to help bring those people back home."

"Yeah, that would be nice. Do you think Saran Airlines would do that if someone asks?"

"I don't know," I said, "I really don't know."

"Do you think they would agree if you ask them Dad?"

"Why would they? I am sure it would cost them a lot of money to send a ship over. With all the travel restrictions imposed, I am sure they are suffering financially, and to expect them to send a boat to rescue people at this time would be foolish."

Archana went back to her phone and tapped around a little bit more.

"Aha, look at this. On their website they talk about corporate social responsibility. They are saying that they have donated large sums of money to help the families of their employees cope with job losses and the loss of family members due to the pandemic. They also claim to do their part to reduce the emissions from the various modes of transport that they offer by adopting the latest technological innovations designed to reduce carbon emissions."

"Well, Saran Airlines has always taken good care of their employees and ensure that their needs are addressed. It was a good company to work for. But these people are not their employees, nor do they have any connection to Saran Airlines."

Archana put her phone away. "Anyway Dad, it's not our concern. We have no power over Saran Airlines. It seems absurd to think that the airlines would consider doing this just because a former employee wants to help some people completely unrelated to them."

"Hmm."

After a while, Archana left the room, and I decided to bring the idea up to Kiran when I saw him on the way to my next therapy session.

The next day, Ramani and Manoj helped me get ready for my therapy session as usual. They fed me and helped me get into comfortable clothes and shoes. Then they took me down to the van once it arrived to take me to therapy. The last few times, Ramani and Archana had not joined me at the clinic; they just waited for me at home.

The van left my apartment complex and drove to the shopping complex where Kiran usually got in. The van stopped, the nurse stepped out and Kiran sat down next to me. The van started moving again.

"Hello sir, how are you?" Kiran asked, smiling as he put his seat belt on.

"I am good Kiran, how are you?"

"I am doing well sir. How is your therapy going?"

"It is going okay. The doctor said that, in today's session, they are going to increase the intensity of the therapy to see how my body responds."

"Ah okay. Hope that helps you even more, sir. Good luck with that."

"Thanks Kiran. Do you have more statements for us to review?"

"Today I don't have any statements sir, but I wanted to tell you that so far, you have helped us identify fraudulent transactions amounting to ₹20 million. Around ₹16 million of that has happened during the pandemic when business was down everywhere. The people who stole did so because they were desperate, and in some cases because they were just greedy."

"Oh, that is good to know Kiran. I am happy that I have been helpful."

"Most definitely sir. You have been more than helpful. I have been using all the methods you have been teaching me in preparing training materials so that the whole accounting team can use your techniques to detect fraud more efficiently."

"Good...good. So, what is the plan now? What can I help with?"

"There is a big project that I wanted to discuss with you sir. We would like your help with it, but I am not sure if it will be possible."

"Kiran, before we talk about that, I wanted to ask if I can get some kind of compensation for the work I have done so far? Do you think Mr. Saran would be willing to do that?"

"Yes, of course Mr. Niyogi. Mr. Saran has personally asked me to find out how you would like to be compensated."

"That is nice of him. I will think about that and get back to you. In the meantime, I wanted to ask you some more questions."

"Yes sir, ask me anything."

"Since the pandemic started, I am sure a lot of the company's trips must have been cancelled, right?"

"Yes sir, a lot of them."

"Now that the pandemic is showing signs of slowing down, do you expect all the cancelled trips to start up again?"

"We surely are hoping so, sir. Especially since we have put in an order for a couple of large cruise ships and some smaller passenger boats that are expected to be delivered this year. The way the contracts were written up, we can't even cancel those orders. Of course, the manufacturers allowed us to cancel some of the larger orders because they were also facing supply-chain issues, but some boats are going to get delivered soon."

"Okay. I know from back in my days with the company that when new aircraft arrived they used to do a promotional tour with people from the media, some select guests and such. Are those still done?"

"If the pandemic was not around, they would have surely been done for the boats we are buying, but now I am not sure. It is difficult to get people to travel by boat again, especially since so many COVID outbreaks happened on boats. Why do you ask sir?"

"I have never been on a boat; I mean, at least not one that was moving. Long ago when I went to Mangaluru with my family, I went on a tour of a large cargo boat, but that boat was docked in the port."

"Well, if that is what you want, I will find out if we can get you on a boat trip sir."

"Thank you, Kiran. I will think about that and let you know. Now tell me about this big project you mentioned." Just as I said that, the van came to a stop.

"Oh, we are at the clinic sir. I will let you carry on with your therapy and I'll see you on the way back. We can talk more then!" Kiran got out of the van, and the nurse took me into the clinic for my therapy.

"Hello Mr. Niyogi, how are you feeling today?" asked Dr. Reddy, walking towards me with a clipboard in hand. "As we discussed last time, we want to up the intensity today to see if we can see a corresponding increase in the positive effects of the session. Are you still okay for us to try that?"

"Yes...doctor," I said, suddenly wishing Archana and Ramani were there. "Ah, Dr. Reddy, can you call my daughter and inform her that you are increasing the intensity?"

"Yes, of course we will. We will start the session only after getting confirmation from your daughter as well."

I waited for the doctor to speak to Archana and come back. After five minutes, Dr. Reddy returned. "Your daughter said that she agrees. But since your daughter and wife are not here today, we will only increase the intensity slightly."

"Okay."

At the end of the biking session, I was tired, sweaty and breathing hard, but it was not any more tiring than the previous times. It felt like they had not increased the speed by much.

The impulse-therapy session however, felt very different, as I could feel that the impulses were sharper. I came out of the session feeling a lot more energetic than usual.

After the sessions, I thanked the staff, and the nurse again wheeled me to the van. Kiran was already waiting inside as usual.

"How are you feeling after the session sir?" he asked once the van started moving.

"I feel good. It was tiring, but overall, I feel good. You were saying something about a big project?"

"Yes. In the run-up to Saran Airlines going public, there is going to be an external audit of the company by KPMG. Mr. Saran wants us to do an internal audit before that happens so we can ensure that there are no surprises during the KPMG audit."

"What areas will the audit cover?" I asked.

"It will mainly be a thorough audit of our internal control processes and the organization's ability to prevent fraud. The goal will be to recommend separation of duties, roles and responsibilities, staff rotation and documentation. All the company's departments will be going through the audit, including the finance department."

"That is going to be big project! How can I help?"

"Well sir, we want to review all the financial reports, audit the documentation that is being recorded at all levels and ensure that we have a system in place that leaves a paper trail of all steps of every financial transaction. I need help to prepare a plan for the audit to ensure that we don't miss anything important."

"Okay, I will be happy to help. When do you want to start?"

"As soon as possible sir."

"Okay. Give me some time to think, and the next time we meet, I will try to give you a checklist to get started with."

"Thank you, sir. I am not sure if I am asking too much from you sir," said Kiran. "I hope it is not going to put too much strain on you. I don't want to ask any more than what is possible for you."

"Writing things down is still a challenge for me Kiran, so is reading, so I am not sure how much more useful I can be with the planning, but I will try."

For the rest of the ride back home, I kept thinking about how I could help with this new project. If I had all my faculties and could work without any impairments, I would have been able to research the latest rules and regulations that governed internal audits and then come up with a plan. But with all the difficulty I was having with reading and writing, I did not know what I could do to help.

Chapter 13 - Mr. Niyogi

Last night my sleep was restless. I woke up many times and had to wake Manoj up to help me go to the bathroom. It was hard to get up and walk to the bathroom by myself. My feet kept getting lock up. I would start taking some steps, and then my legs would just refuse to move. My knee would move slightly forward and my heel would raise of the floor a bit, but the front of my foot would not move from the ground.

My upper body would lean forward expecting my feet to follow, but my feet would not lift off the floor, causing me to start falling forward many times. Usually someone would always be with me when I was walking. They would hold me if I was in danger of falling over. Manoj, Ramani or Archana would be there to keep me upright.

But last night I woke Manoj up so many times to take me to the bathroom, so when I woke up in the morning, I decided to use the walls for support and walk to the bathroom myself. I pushed myself off the bed, held on to the wall to steady myself and started to push my feet forward. I really needed to go to the bathroom, so I pushed myself, and my feet moved. Whenever my feet refused to lift of the floor, I slid them forward instead.

I made it to the bathroom door, held on to the frame with one hand and opened the door with the other. I stepped in and held on to the door handle so I could get close to the toilet. The sight of the toilet increased my need to go. I shuffled forward as quickly as I could and managed to pull my shorts down and sit on the toilet just in time.

After I was finished, I used the hand-held bidet to clean myself. I got up, and with one hand holding the door, I pulled up my shorts. I shuffled to the door of the bathroom and used the door frame to pull myself out with one hand. My next step would have been out of the bathroom, but my feet froze.

My leg kept twitching, but my feet refused to move. After much convincing, my left foot moved a few inches, and then my right one moved a few inches. My upper body leaned forward expecting my left foot to move again, but it did not. I had stepped away from the door, and my body started leaning forward. My right hand was still holding the door frame, but my fingers did not have the strength to steady me. I started losing my hold on the door frame as I kept leaning forward. I started to panic, my eyes on the floor in front of me.

At last, my fingers lost all contact with the door frame, and the next thing I heard was my own howl as I fell forward. My forehead made contact with the marble flooring, and a few seconds later, I felt a searing pain in my left shoulder. I let out an even louder howl.

I could hear hurried footsteps and panicked voices. I felt hands turning me over and lifting me; someone touched my left hand, sending another spike of pain through my body, and I yelled again. I could hear voices, but I did not hear what they were saying. The pain was just too much to bear, and then everything went dark.

I woke up inside a van. It must have been going really fast because I could feel the bumps on the road in my body. Ramani was beside me in the van, and so was Manoj.

"Where are we going?" I asked Ramani.

"To the hospital," she said.

"Why?" I asked. No sooner had I spoken than I immediately started to feel a throbbing pain in my left side. I tried to move and felt another spike of pain.

"You fell, and something happened to your left arm. We are going to the emergency room," Ramani said.

The pain was so overwhelming that I couldn't say anything for the rest of the ride. The van reached the hospital, and the door opened. The stretcher that I was on got pulled out, and I was moved onto a gurney. I was quickly taken into the hospital, and what followed was a series of tests, X-rays and ultrasounds. I was then moved to a bed in the emergency room, where I waited for the doctor.

Ramani was next to me, and so was Archana.

"How is the pain Dad?" asked Archana. "I came as soon as I could."

There was an IV line running from a bag hanging next to the bed into my right arm. It must have been a pain killer because I could not feel the pain in my left arm. I felt good.

"There is no pain my dear," I said. At least at that moment, I did not feel anything.

"How did it happen?" asked Archana, speaking to Ramani. I was also looking at Ramani, waiting for her to answer.

"I think your dad went to the bathroom by himself; he did not wake up Manoj or me. We heard him falling and then yelling," said Ramani, gently patting my right arm. "By the time I came into the room, Manoj was already there trying to turn him onto his back. He must have fallen onto his left side; his arm was folded under him. After Manoj turned him over, I could see the swelling on his left shoulder."

"Did you call an ambulance?"

"Manoj called 102, and within a short while a van arrived. They came up with the stretcher, and all three of us came to the hospital in the van."

"Okay. Stay here. I will go find out what happened with the test results," said Archana, and she went towards the nurse's station.

Ramani and I waited for Archana to come back, and after a while she returned with a doctor walking beside her.

"Mr. Niyogi, your left shoulder is dislocated. It must have happened when you fell. We are going to perform a closed reduction first; that is, we will try and push the joint back into the socket. It will hurt a little bit. We have given you a mild sedative, but we may have to give you another local anesthetic. We are waiting for the chief to come; there are obviously some risks involved, since you are taking Parkinson's medication. Plus your age has to be considered."

"What are the risks, doctor?" asked Archana.

"Well, the effects of anaesthesia combined with the kind of medication he is on can be very hard on a person of your dad's age. So, we have to pick the right anesthetic. Or we have to do this without the anaesthesia. The chief of emergency will decide."

Ramani was squeezing my right arm, whether to reassure me or to reassure herself, I did not know.

"How long will...the recovery take?" I asked the doctor.

"It is very hard to say sir; it depends. Younger people with no health complications may need four to six weeks to resume normal light activities and three to six months before they can go back to their normal routine. In your case, it is hard to say. But don't worry sir; we will get you back home very soon."

I needed to be home soon. I had to get back to resume my therapy; that was the only way I could continue working with Kiran. I had to finish that project soon. There was not much time left. If this injury locked me up in the house for six weeks, or worse, for six months, I didn't know what I would do.

After an hour of waiting, the doctor who had come to talk to me earlier walked in with another doctor.

"This is Mr. Niyogi. This is his wife Mrs. Ramani and his daughter Mrs. Archana," he told the new doctor. "Mr. Niyogi, this is the chief of emergency.”

The chief of emergency looked at the charts that were handed to him and read through my medical history. This was the hospital I usually went to, so they had all my case notes.

“Mr. Niyogi, we have to be careful when administering anaesthetics, given your age and the medication that you are taking. Are you okay to go through the procedure without anaesthesia? To be frank, we may not have much of a choice.”

“Will it hurt a lot, doctor?” asked Archana.

“The closed reduction is not as painful as surgery, but it will hurt nonetheless. Are you okay with us going ahead without a sedative?”

“I...am not sure,” said Archana, who seemed to be struggling with making the decision. One option would cause me unimaginable pain, and the other posed great risk. “What do you think Dad?”

She reached out and held my right hand. I wanted to get out of the hospital with my wits still intact if possible. “Hmm, okay, go ahead without the anesthetic,” I said.

The chief did not wait for further confirmation. He nodded his head towards the attending doctor and told him to go ahead. I am sure he had other patients to get to and did not usually delve into decisions too much once they were made. That is what I would have done if I were in his place.

The attending doctor took a deep breath and let out a sigh. “I don’t like it, but this is the way we have to go. Please hang tight; I will be back to transfer you to the orthopaedic operating room and will call an orthopaedic surgeon to come and do the reduction.”

It took another couple of hours before the doctor was back with a team of nurses. They had a gurney with them. The doctor asked Ramani and Archana to stand back, and he and three other nurses efficiently moved me to the gurney. It must have been their expertise or the pain killers, but I did not feel any discomfort while they moved me.

Just then Ramani remembered that I had not consumed any food that morning; in fact, I had had nothing since the previous night.

"Doctor, my husband has not had anything to eat since his dinner last night. In the rush to come to the hospital we completely forgot about it," she said.

"It may not be a bad thing," the doctor said. "If he eats now, it may be a while before we can do the procedure, as the pain might cause him to throw up. This should not take more than an hour; we can feed him as soon as this is done."

"Oh okay. But won't having some food in him give him additional strength to withstand the pain?" Ramani suggested.

"Maybe, but we have to go now, otherwise we lose the operating room, and we don't know when it will become available again."

Ramani looked crestfallen hearing that. I looked at her and said, "It's okay Ramani; I can wait."

She stepped back from the gurney reluctantly, and I was wheeled away towards the operating room. Ramani and Archana followed us closely. After reaching the operating room, Ramani and Archana were asked to wait outside, and the nurses held open the double doors to the operating room. I was wheeled in, and the doors were closed behind me.

I was once again shifted, this time to the operating bed, which was in the middle of the room. The orthopaedic surgeon was already looking at the X-rays and the ultrasounds on his computer. He asked his own assistants to step in, and the nurses that had brought me to the room stepped back. The attending doctor from the emergency room left after instructing them to call him if required.

All in all, there were four people around me, two on either side.

"Mr. Niyogi, this is going to hurt a lot. Please bite down on this bite guard so you don't accidentally bite your tongue." I opened my mouth so they could insert the bite guard, then I bit down on it.

The two nurses on my right side held on to me. Their grip was firm but not overly hard. The doctor gently lifted my arm, and I started to feel the pain in spite of the pain killers. The doctor was carefully feeling the socket and the joint to determine the right place to apply pressure. Even his light touch was sending waves of pain through my shoulder.

I was moaning into the bite guard.

"We have to be quick about this," the doctor said to his team.

He then started applying pressure onto the joint while moving my arm into the correct position. The pain shot through the roof. I thrashed my legs on the bed; I was pulling on the bed sheets with my right hand and might have ripped the sheets if my hand was not held down by the nurses on my right.

The pressure on my shoulder joint kept on increasing along with the pain, then suddenly, the excruciating pain was gone, replaced by a dull, mild pain.

"Okay, we are done Mr. Niyogi. Your joint is back in its place," said the doctor, gently folding my left hand across my chest. "Raise the bed," he said to the nurses.

The top half of the bed rose slowly until I was in a seated position. The nurses quickly and gently eased my left hand into a shoulder sling to support my arm. They then smoothly shifted me back onto the gurney that had been used to bring me into the room.

I was spent. I was so exhausted that my eyes were falling shut. I could barely feel the gurney moving, and with much difficulty, I kept trying to open my eyes. I caught glimpses of the hallways and overhead lights as the gurney was wheeled back to the ER.

After I was back in the same spot as before, I saw Ramani and Archana walk in. They were both looking at my left arm and the sling it was in.

"Are you okay Dad? Was the pain too much?" asked Archana. "We heard you from outside the room."

I did not say anything. I just nodded and reached out to hold Ramani's hand.

"We have asked for some food to be given to you. They will be here any minute," said Ramani, always worrying about my food.

After a few minutes, a woman wearing white overalls, a white hairnet and white gloves arrived pushing a cart. She started preparing a large syringe with a greenish liquid. She then connected the syringe to my feeding tube and proceeded to inject all of the liquid into it.

I could feel the liquid slowly filling up my stomach. I did not feel it right away, but within ten minutes, I could feel a slight surge of energy as my body started digesting the food. Once the woman disconnected the syringe from the tube, I noticed that the adult diaper I was wearing was completely full. I could feel the wetness on my skin.

I told Ramani about it, and she had someone come and change the diaper. I could no longer stay awake and fell into a deep sleep.

"Mr. Niyogi," I heard someone say, "are you sleeping? I hope you don't forget about us; about me."

"Huh, who?" I whispered when I opened my eyes. The room I was now in was almost dark, and Archana was sleeping on a bed next to me.

"Mr. Niyogi, are you going to get back to trying to help us? You have not done much yet. You have not even asked your ex-employer to come and rescue us. When are you going to ask them?"

"Are you crazy? Don't you see I have just had a fall and have injured my shoulder? How do you think I can go and meet anyone and ask anything?"

"You are very lucky, Mr. Niyogi. If anything happens to you, there are people around you who will immediately do everything they can to help you. But that is not the case with us. There is no one to help us here. It is just us on the island suffering without any help. We put our faith in you, and you are doing nothing."

"I can't do anything right now; I am stuck here. I have to get at least a bit better and get home. Only then will I be able to do something. How can you not see that?"

"I cannot see anything, Mr. Niyogi. I am not there in Bengaluru, remember? I am stuck on this remote island."

I did not respond; I had nothing to say. I tried to close both my ears with my hands. Forgetting that my left arm was in a sling, I tried lifting it to my ear, and a sharp pain shot through my shoulder. I bit my lip, trying to suppress my moan so as not to wake up Archana.

Chapter 14 - Mr. Niyogi

I woke up a few more times during the night, woken by the same voice that had been troubling me for the past few weeks. The same voice, which I believed belonged to a young man stuck on an island far away waiting for me to do something to rescue him.

Every time I woke up, Archana would open her eyes and get up from the bed she was sleeping on to come to my side and ask if I wanted anything. Considering how disturbed my sleep was, it seemed to me that she did not sleep at all, as she remained alert to even the sounds my bed made every time I shifted due to the pain.

And when the sun rose the next morning, she was up. She went to freshen up and then sat with me while we waited for the doctor to come and speak to us.

The nurses came a bit later and gave me my liquid breakfast. Archana went to the cafeteria to grab a quick breakfast and coffee, then she was back by my side.

"Archana, dear, aren't you going to the office today?" I asked her.

"No Dad. I asked for some time off so I can be here with you until you are back home."

"Okay." *Thank you, my dear daughter. Having you by my side makes me less nervous about being in this hospital.* "I hate hospitals. I want to go home."

"Yes Dad, hopefully very soon. We will wait for the doctor to come, and we can ask him when we can go home."

And so, we waited. An hour, two hours, and three hours—and finally the doctor came.

"Mr. Niyogi, I will be monitoring your case today," the doctor said while checking the sling and then gently prodding my shoulder joint. "How are you doing today?"

"I am okay...there is still pain, but it's not much," I said.

The doctor carefully pulled my arm out of the sling and asked me to move the arm up and down and then from side to side. I gritted my teeth and did my best to complete the movements. The pain must have shown up on my face, as the doctor then said, "We will keep you here for one more day, okay? If your movement improves a little bit, we will send you home tomorrow. Okay?"

"Okay..." I said, feeling dejected. I looked at Archana and she nodded, telling me that it was okay.

The doctor left. Archana followed him out of the room and closed the door behind her, but the door did not close fully.

"Doctor, what could have caused him to fall?" I heard her asking the doctor.

"Well, I am sure you must have seen this happen before. It is not uncommon for Parkinson's patients to suddenly find themselves unable to take a step forward. That is what I think happened here. He must have been walking and his feet froze, but his body kept moving with the momentum, so he fell."

"Is his arm going to be okay? He uses both hands to support himself usually."

"The ultrasounds show that there is some displacement in the muscles and tissues around his shoulder. At his age and because of his condition, it could be a while before he regains enough strength in this shoulder to be able to use his left arm to support himself.

"Falls like these are indications of advancement of Parkinson's. You should watch out for him more going forward. I will arrange a consultation with the palliative care department. Talk to them about how to manage your father's care. As you know, there is no known cure for Parkinson's."

"Okay doctor."

Archana then came into the room and tried to put on a cheerful face.

"The doctor said that you will be better soon Dad. He said that your hand will heal well."

"Hmm," I said with a smile. I did not want to tell her that I could hear her conversation with the doctor.

"The doctor asked us to go to the palliative care department for a consultation."

"Doesn't palliative care mean end of life care, Archana?" I asked.

"No Dad, palliative care has several forms, and end of life care is one of them. For you, we are going to find out what can be done to manage the symptoms of Parkinson's, that's all."

"Hmm."

I sat quietly for a bit. If I was nearing my end, I could not wait much longer. I had to get back to work, and the only way I could do that was with Archana's help. There was no other way I could manage what I was planning.

I kept wondering how to broach the subject with Archana for the next two hours. I was getting nowhere. I could not think of a good way to bring it up to her. There was nothing that I could say that would make this part easier.

On the other hand, I had nothing to lose. Well, that was not true. I did have something to lose: my ability to help rescue those people on the island. But other than that, there was nothing to lose, and the rescue was a remote possibility anyway. I had not brought this up with Saran Airlines yet, and for all practical purposes, they might just say that they cannot help in this matter.

"Archana," I said, turning my head towards her. She was on her phone, her reading glasses perched on her nose. "Can I tell you something?"

"Yes Dad, what's up?" she asked, putting her phone down and looking at me over her glasses.

"I have been keeping a secret from you and your mom."

"What do you mean 'secret?' What secrets do you have from us Dad?" She seemed slightly amused at the notion.

"I have been doing some work for Saran Airlines in the last few weeks."

"Ha ha, very funny Dad," said Archana and picked up her phone again.

"I have been meeting with Kiran on the way to therapy. He gets into the clinic's van after it picks me up and then waits somewhere while I'm in therapy. Then he joins me in the van again on the way back."

"You are kidding." Archana looked doubtful. "How did you manage that? And how does Kiran manage to get into the clinic's van?"

"I don't know how he managed it; maybe he has connections at the clinic. He brings documents for me to review, some statements, and we work on those on the way to the clinic and back."

"Are you serious Dad? You are not joking?"

"No, my dear. I am serious."

"Oh my God, really? I have so many questions. First of all, why do you need to do this? Aren't you retired?" She started pacing next to the bed and was getting angrier by the second. "How could Saran Airlines ask you to do this work knowing your condition? Why did you not let us know earlier? And—"

"Come and sit down here first. I can't keep turning my head; my neck and shoulder hurts," I said. Archana immediately sat down on the end of the bed.

"Okay, now tell me, why does Saran Airlines need you to work for them? Don't they have regular employees?"

"Well, they did not ask me...I asked them if I could do some work."

"But why? Aren't you sick and in pain all the time? Why do you want to take the trouble?"

"I am sick....I am sick of being sick all the time. I was happier when I was working and when I was healthy. Now all I am is a burden on you and Ramani and everyone in the family," I said, "and I know there is no cure for Parkinson's. There is no getting better for me. I wanted to do something so I could feel like I can still be useful to someone, even now."

Archana calmed down a bit and said, "Don't think like that Dad; you are not a burden to us. We love you and we want to make sure that you are as comfortable as possible. I am sure it is not easy for you to deal with everything that is happening to your body and mind. I know that you have always wanted to be the one to take care of us."

"And that is why I wanted to do this work. And I helped them to find close to ₹20 million that was lost due to fraud committed by some former employees."

"That is amazing Dad; that is truly something. No wonder Kiran was singing your praises when he came to visit all those weeks ago. Okay, so you helped them, which is great. How did that make you feel?"

"Well, it felt good of course. I felt like I was useful again; like I still have a lot to give."

Archana leaned forward and kissed my forehead. "That is good Dad; as long as you are happy."

"The work is not done yet...there is a major audit that needs to happen, and I need to work on that," I said, afraid of what Archana was going to say next.

"What do you mean there is more work? You have helped them find ₹20 million; what more could they want?"

"They don't want anything more from me, but I want to do more."

Archana shook her head. "I still don't fully understand why you want to go to all that trouble. It's not like you need the money, if they are offering you money, and you just dislocated your shoulder. Aren't you in pain?"

"Archana, I don't know what else I can tell you to convince you, but in spite of everything I am going through, I still want to help with this project."

"What will Mom say? Have you told her about this?"

"I haven't told her yet, and I don't want to. She is already under a lot of stress worrying about my health. I don't want to put her under more stress. As much as I want to do this, I don't know if I will have the courage if your Mom is completely against it."

"What about me? Have you thought about how worried I would be if you are doing something that might affect your health?"

"I did not want to trouble you any more than I already have, and that is why I kept it hidden from you too all this time. But now I need your help, and there is no one else I can ask."

Archana's shoulders dropped, and she went to stand in the middle of the room facing me. She did not say anything for a minute or so and then started pacing the room again. This time she seemed to be deep in thought.

Eventually she came over to the bed and sat down on the edge again. "Okay Dad. What do you want to do? What do you need from me?"

"I want to go away from home for a couple of weeks; stay in a hotel or something. I'll ask Kiran to bring the files to the hotel, then we can work together until the audit is done."

"Dad, even when you were working there as an employee before your retirement, you never went away for so long for work. How are we going to convince Mom?"

"Well...we may have to lie to her. We say that I have to stay at the hospital for two weeks and that I have to be in isolation, so no one can visit me."

Archana burst out laughing. "She is definitely not going to believe that Dad! There is no way that will work."

"We have to try; we won't know until we try."

"I have a hard time imagining that she will agree to this. Won't being away from you cause her even more concern?"

"Yes, that might happen, but I need to do this. What can we do?"

"Hmm, let me think about it for a bit. Give me some time."

"Take all the time you need my dear, and sorry for putting you in such a position."

Archana sat down on the bed again and was soon back on her phone. She did not say anything for another half an hour, seemingly lost in thought.

"Okay, I have an idea," she said at last. "We could say that you got COVID while you were at the hospital and that they need to isolate you. And that you will be fully taken care of but will remain in isolation in the hospital for a couple of weeks. But that means that you have to go into this fake isolation as soon as they discharge you."

"Are you confident about this plan? You mom won't suspect any-thing?"

"She might, but it's the best plan I could think of. We will have to send you to this hotel tomorrow if the doctor discharges you tomorrow...but wait a minute. You need so much care Dad. You need Manoj to be with you. I cannot take two weeks off to help you. What if he tells Mom?"

"I can ask for the company to arrange a full-time nurse, and we can have someone from the clinic come and assist me at the hotel. I think the company is going to benefit enough from me that they might arrange for all of this."

"Are you sure Dad? I feel that it is asking a lot from them. They can very easily hire an external consultant to do the audit instead."

"They could, but that would cost them at least ten times the money they would spend on me, even with all the assistance I need."

"Okay Dad. You talk to Kiran and ask him to make the arrangements, and I will try and find the doctor to come and take a look at you again. Here, I will dial Kiran's number so you can talk to him."

Archana dialed Kiran's number on her phone, and when he picked up, she told him that I had asked to speak with him. She then handed me the phone and went out looking for the doctor.

"Hi Kiran," I said.

"Hello Mr. Niyogi," said Kiran.

I proceeded to explain the situation and what Archana and I had discussed. I asked him if he could talk to Mr. Saran and make arrangement for a hotel somewhere close to the hospital where I could stay for two weeks. I also told him that Archana would tell Ramani that I was at the hospital under isolation. That way, I would be available full time to work on the audit for Saran Airlines.

I also told him that we would have to finish the audit within two weeks. I did not tell Kiran about my shoulder injury because I did not want to put him in the tough position of having to make any decisions on my behalf.

Kiran asked me whether I was really sure about going ahead with this, and I assured him that I was. Once he was convinced that I was fully onboard and willing to do this project, he said that he would talk to Mr. Saran and inform Archana about the next steps.

Just as I was finishing the call, Archana walked in with the doctor.

"Hello Mr. Niyogi, how are you feeling now?" he asked.

I handed the phone to Archana and said, "I am doing okay doctor. There is still some pain in my shoulder, but it is not too bad."

"We want to continue to monitor you for a day or two, and then we will do another ultrasound before sending you back home."

"Okay doctor," I said.

After the doctor left, I told Archana about my conversation with Kiran. She nodded and went to sit down on the bed next to mine, engrossed in her phone for a while.

We spent the rest of the day just waiting for the nurses to come in, help me with going to the bathroom, administering medicine, bringing me food, etc. Archana and I also spoke about how to break the news to Ramani so she wouldn't suspect anything.

Chapter 15 - Mr. Niyogi

I waited eagerly for Kiran to call me back. He was supposed to talk to Mr. Saran about getting approval for the hotel booking and also paying for nurses to help me with my needs while I worked alongside Kiran.

Archana went home for a few hours the next morning to fetch me a change of clothes and mainly to convince Ramani that I had COVID and that I had to spend two weeks at the hospital in isolation.

Timing was key if we were going to be able to pull this off. I had to get confirmation from Kiran before I was discharged from the hospital that day so that I could go straight from the hospital to the hotel. If I had to wait another day for a decision from Saran and I had to go home, it would become very difficult for us to find a way for me to get away from the house again.

I was at the hospital in my room waiting for Archana to come back, because there was no way for Kiran to contact me directly. He would have to call Archana and let her know.

I wondered how Ramani was taking the news of my fake COVID diagnosis. The tension of not knowing what was happening outside of my room was killing me. I found the red button that I was to use to call a nurse, and I pressed it.

A few minutes later, a nurse came into the room. She was holding a clipboard in her hands and had left a cart in the hallway outside the door.

"Hello Mr. Niyogi," said the nurse cheerfully; she always seemed to be cheerful. "Did you press the button to call for a nurse?"

"Yes, I did. I wanted to ask if my daughter has returned yet...have you seen her?"

"Oh Mr. Niyogi, no, she has not come back yet. This is the third time you have called one of us to ask about this," she said, checking the bed for any signs of wetness just in case. "Did you need anything that you are hesitating to tell us? You know you can ask for any help from us, right?"

"No, no, I don't need anything right now. I only wanted to know if my daughter has returned yet."

"Okay. Well she has not, and I am sure she will come to see you as soon as she is back. Now, please don't keep calling us unless you really need something. There are a lot of patients on the floor today, and we are all tied up. I am not saying don't call us at all, I am just saying call us if you need something. Okay?"

I kept my hands away from the button after that. I did not want to risk angering the nurse any further.

"Why did it take so long to get back my dear?" I asked Archana as soon as she walked in. "I have been waiting for so long."

"Sorry Dad, I had to take a bath, and then Kiran called me just as I got out of the bath. I was talking to him for a while, and then I was not sure if I should tell Mom right away. Well anyway, I finally decided not to tell her anything yet. I picked up some clothes for you, and I came back."

"Okay. What did Kiran say?"

"I don't know if I would call it good news, but he said that Mr. Saran agreed to put you up in the hotel and also pay for the nurses and any other expenses. He said that, as per their calculations, the total cost still adds up to way below what they would have to pay an external auditor."

"Hmm, that is good news," I said, "so what is the plan now? What are we going to say to your mom, and when do we go to the hotel?"

"Let's wait a few hours, and then I will tell Mom that they did a COVID test after finding you feverish, and that you need to be isolated given everything else that you have going on with your health. I will say that you need to be isolated for two weeks."

"Sorry my dear, for putting you through this."

"Well...it's okay Dad. I hope it is all worth it. I hope that your health does not get affected by this stunt. I won't know what to say to Mom if that happens."

"Put it on me; tell her that I made you do it."

"You *are* making me do this, and I won't be lying if I say that," said Archana, laughing.

I smiled. "I am glad you are helping me; I will be less nervous with your help."

"Just don't say anything else, or I may change my mind."

I was discharged from the hospital later that evening, and we went through the myriad formalities of getting discharged. Archana drove me from the hospital and then parked on the side of the road after going a few blocks.

She pulled out her phone and said, "It's time to call Mom and tell her. Are you ready?"

I nodded.

"Don't say anything, okay? Remember, you are in the isolation ward right now," she said. Then she dialed Ramani's number. "Mom, I have some good news and some bad news...which do you want to hear first?" Archana put the phone on speaker.

"Tell me the bad news first," said Ramani.

"Dad tested positive for COVID, and the doctors said that he must remain in isolation for two weeks in the COVID ward," said Archana. We waited with bated breath to see what Ramani would say.

"What? When? How could this happen? What about you? Why isolation, can't they just send him home and he can isolate here?" Ramani sounded extremely concerned.

"Mom, slow down. Given his recent dislocation, they said that he is very weak and it is best if he is isolated in the hospital so that any immediate care can be given to him if needed. And somehow, I tested negative. They have already taken him into the ward and did not give us any options."

"What? Archana, how could they do that? I want to talk to the doctor; they can't do that without letting us know first."

"Mom, they said it is part of their COVID protocols. And the doctor seemed pretty adamant. I already asked them all these questions."

"I want to talk to your father; how can I talk to him?"

"We can talk to him tomorrow morning. I will come back to the hospital and give them my phone so that they can pass it on to him. You can call him then."

"How is he going to manage, Archana? Will they take good care of him? Now, I want to see him. Come home and take me to see your father."

I was getting worried that Ramani was not going to accept this story easily.

"Ma, relax," Archana said. "He is in good hands; there is nothing to worry about. The hospital will take good care of him. It will be okay."

"I should have been there at the hospital..."

"Mom, it's okay. Don't worry about it. He will be fine. He will be back home before long. Okay? Listen, I have to go; the doctor is calling me. I will come see you later, okay?"

"Okay, but wait...what is the good news?"

"Ah! The good news is that his arm is doing okay. His shoulder will heal."

"Hmm, okay. Call me and tell me what the doctor tells you."

Archana hung up and turned to me. "Dad, I hope you are happy you made me tell such a big lie to Mom."

"I am sorry my dear..."

Archana let out a big sigh and said, "It's okay Dad. Let's get you to the hotel. I will call Kiran."

Archana spoke to Kiran, and he gave her the name of the hotel they had reserved. Archana then drove me to the hotel and checked me in at reception. She also requested a wheelchair.

Someone came to the car with the wheelchair, and Archana then helped me get into it before taking me up to the room. We settled in and waited for Kiran to arrive.

"Kiran said that he will be here by six or so," Archana told me.

"Okay my dear."

While we were waiting, Archana put my clothes in the closet and my toothbrush in the bathroom. She had also brought a bunch of adult diapers that she put near the clothes, in case I found it hard to control my bowels.

She then came and sat down next to me. She kept checking her phone every few minutes and occasionally bit her nails while we waited for Kiran to arrive.

Eventually there was a knock on the door, and when Archana opened it, Kiran walked in with a nurse.

"Hello Mr. Niyogi, hello Archana, how are you?" he said. "This is Ravi. Ravi, this is Mr. Niyogi. You will be taking care of him for the next two weeks."

"Hello sir," said Ravi.

"Ravi will be staying in the room next to yours and will come to you whenever you need help. He will also be with us all the time to help with your food and any other needs. We've also arranged for a therapist who will be available in the daytime to provide you with some physical therapy as needed. Is there anything else that you need sir?"

"No Kiran, thank you. Are we starting work in the morning?"

"Yes sir, let's start in the morning. I will collect all the documents from the office, and we have booked a conference room for us to work in. I will bring everything to the room tomorrow, and Ravi will help you to get ready and take you there."

"Okay Kiran. I will be ready in the morning."

Kiran showed me how to intimate to Ravi that I needed assistance, and then he unlocked the door that connected my room with the adjoining one where Ravi would be staying.

Ravi then left the room, and Kiran was about to leave too when Archana stopped him.

"Kiran," said Archana, "thank you for doing all of this to help my dad, and thank you for personally handling all of these arrangements. I understand that my dad wants to help you and that his contribution will help Saran Airlines a lot, but I am worried about his health."

"I understand Archana. I am also worried about Mr. Niyogi's health, and I will do my best to ensure that he has everything he needs while he is here with me. And I will keep sending you updates. You can call me whenever you want to talk to him, or you can call the hotel room, or you can even come over whenever you want. Hopefully we will be done with the audit sooner rather than later."

"Okay. Well, thank you. Please let me know if there is an emergency. I will come right over."

"Will do."

After Kiran left, Archana came over to me and said, "Dad, I want you to be very careful. Call Ravi for going to the washroom or anywhere; accept his help. Don't hesitate. Don't try to walk for too long without help. Use the wheelchair, okay? I want to stay here with you, but I can't. Mom will be expecting me. I now have to go face her."

Archana then left, and I was alone in the room for a while. I had completely forgotten about the pain in my shoulder with all the excitement going on. And now that I was alone, I started to feel the pain creeping up on me again.

What have I gotten myself into? There is no one here with me. If I was at home, Ramani or Manoj or Archana would have given me pain killers for the pain. I don't know what I will do now if the pain keeps increasing.

I tried to ignore my pain and tried to fall asleep, but a familiar voice woke me up.

"Mr. Niyogi, don't forget about me in your sleep. Are you going to come to the island soon?"

"Huh...I am trying," I said, "I am trying my best. It is not easy for me. I don't know if you can see my condition, but it is not easy for me. I am doing my best to bring help to you. You have to wait for a few more weeks."

"A few more weeks? I don't know if I can...we can...hold on for a few more weeks. Our rations are running out. We are getting sick."

"I know; I am trying. Please hold on for a bit longer. Give me just a little bit more time."

"Please hurry Mr. Niyogi, please hurry." And just like that, I could see the voice taking the shape of a man. *How could that be? How can this boy be at the island and here in my room at the same time?*

The man kept coming closer and closer until he was within touching distance. I reached out to him, and strangely, I could feel the voice's hand. The man came closer still and gently put his other hand on my shoulder.

The voice then changed a little bit. "Mr. Niyogi? Did you need anything? You said you needed a little time. Is there anything I can help you with?"

Suddenly I realized that it was someone else altogether standing next to me. "Who are you? What are you doing in this room?" I asked, pulling my hand away.

"Sir, I am Ravi, the nurse, here to take care of you. I am staying in the next room. I heard you speak, so I came to see what you needed. Is there anything I can do to help? Do you need anything?"

I looked around. I was not sure what was happening. Then I remembered Ravi, the nurse who had come in with Kiran.

"Ah...Ravi...my shoulder hurts. Do you have a pain killer?"

"I will check sir; I think there is a pain killer amongst your medication."

Ravi then found and took out a vial of a liquid pain killer, which he injected into my feeding tube using a syringe. I could see the pink liquid making its way into the tube.

"Thank you, Ravi."

"I am right next door sir. The connecting door is open. If you call my name, I will hear it, and I will come right away. Do you need to go to the bathroom?"

I said yes, and Ravi took me to the bathroom before helping me back into the bed. I must have fallen asleep immediately, and the next thing I remember was waking up again after a while. I did not know how long I had slept, but lying down was getting painful, and I called out to Manoj to help me sit up.

"Manoj...Manoj...I need to sit up. Manoj, I need to sit up!" I called out.

Manoj did not come, but in a minute or so Ravi did, and he helped me sit up. I kept going back to sleep again and waking up. Every time, I would ask Ravi to help me sit up before falling back asleep again. The long night passed like that until I could see rays of sunlight lighting up the floor and then filling the whole room.

Ravi then helped me go to the bathroom and take in some food and water through the feeding tube. Then he helped me change into a fresh set of clothes. I was now ready to start working. I wanted to start and finish the audit as soon as possible. Then I could ask for the help that I was after.

It must have been after 10 a.m. when I heard a knock on the door and saw Kiran walk in with a briefcase.

135

Chapter 16 - Mr. Niyogi

"I think the work is ready to be shared with Mr. Saran," said Kiran after completing a second read of the report that we wrote up after completing the almost two weeks of work. "I am happy with the way this has turned out sir; what do you think?"

"Yes, I think so too. It looks good. Good work on polishing it all up to such good quality, Kiran."

"Ah, I did nothing sir; it was mostly you. It would not have been possible without you. I am sure it was a difficult two weeks for you, sir."

"With all the services that the company provided me with here at the hotel to accommodate all my needs, it was manageable."

"We are happy to do our part sir. I will wrap things up here, and then I will go and hand over the report to Mr. Saran. I am sure you must be eager to get back home yourself!"

"I can't wait to go home; it has been too long. I want to go and show Ramani that I am okay and that she need not worry about me anymore."

"Well sir, do you want me to call Archana so she can come and pick you up?"

"Uhhh, before we do that Kiran...I want to talk to Mr. Saran. I want to ask him for something," I said.

"Ah yes, of course sir. It is time Saran Airlines gave you your remuneration for all this work. The fraud detection and this audit. I think the company owes you a lot of money sir. You should ask for a lot; you deserve it."

"Well, that is why I want to go see Mr. Saran. Do you think he will have time to see me this afternoon?"

"Hmm, it is 1 p.m. now. Let me do this sir: I will pack up here and quickly head to the office and hand this report over to him. I will also explain the work and show him that it is complete. I will then do my best to get an appointment for you to see him this afternoon. You can stay here if you want while I pack up, or I can ask Ravi to take you back to your room and you can get some rest while you wait. What do you prefer?"

"I will go back to my room, and I will call Archana from there."

"Of course, sir. Ravi," said Kiran, "can you please take Mr. Niyogi back to the room and also help him make a call to his daughter?"

Ravi came over to my chair, unlocked the wheels, and picked up the bag with my medicine and medical equipment. Then he wheeled me out of the room towards the elevator. We got to my room, and after taking me to the bathroom, Ravi helped me get into bed and opened the curtains wide to let some light in.

"Shall I call your daughter now sir?" he asked me.

"Yes, call my daughter."

Ravi picked up the hotel phone and dialed the number, which he knew well at this point, as I had been speaking to Archana most nights I stayed at the hotel. He waited for the call to be picked up and said, "Hello Archana, this is Ravi from the hotel. Mr. Niyogi wanted to speak with you." He then handed the phone to me.

"Dad?" I heard Archana's voice say, "How are you? Is everything okay?"

"Yes, my dear, everything is okay. I called to tell you that my work here is done. We completed the project, and Kiran is going to take the report to Mr. Saran."

"Oh, that is great news Dad! How are you feeling?"

"I feel fine. It took a while, but we finally finished the audit with one day to spare. Now all that I need to do is meet with Mr. Saran once. I want to ask him for something in return for all of this work."

"Oh, wow Dad, good job. I am very happy that you are finally done with this work and that you can come home. Mom has been waiting for you eagerly. How is the pain? Any better?"

"The pain is okay; it is always there; it never leaves me."

"Oh Dad; it will get better. Once you are home, I am sure it will get better. Maybe the bed at the hotel is too soft and does not support you well enough."

"Hmm...enough about my pain my dear. I need you to take me to my meeting with Mr. Saran. I am still waiting to hear what time it will be, but once I do, can you take me please? After the meeting you can take me home."

"Okay Dad. I finish work at 3 p.m. today. So, I can come to the hotel right after to take you. See if the meeting can be arranged for around five-ish so we have enough time to get there."

"Okay, see you soon. Bye," I said to Archana and hung up. "Ravi, Ravi?"

"Yes sir," said Ravi, walking in from the adjoining room.

"Can you please call Kiran? I have not heard back from him yet."

Ravi dialed Kiran's number and handed me the receiver.

"Hello," said Kiran on the other side of the line, "who is this?"

"Kiran, this is Niyogi. Did you get a chance to speak to Mr. Saran yet? Can you ask him if I can see him around five or 5:30 p.m.?"

"Sir, I am still on the way to the office. I should be there soon. I will check if he is free to meet with you around 5 p.m. I will call Ravi and let him know in an hour or two. Is that okay sir?"

"Okay, Kiran. I will wait for your call."

The next two hours dragged on. The minutes and seconds were

moving really slowly. While I was waiting for the call, I tried to take a nap and went to the bathroom a couple of times. Ravi reminded me that I needed to eat, and he fed me my liquefied food through the feeding tube.

Nothing seemed to make the time move forward fast enough.

Then around 2 p.m., Ravi came into the room and said, "Sir, Kiran has called; he wants to talk to you."

"Hello Kiran?" I said, taking the phone eagerly.

"Hello sir! I just spoke to Mr. Saran and showed him the documents that we worked on. He is very impressed with what we have accomplished. He has asked me to thank you for all the work and also agreed to meet with you today at 6 p.m. I can come to the hotel around five to pick you up."

"No, it's okay Kiran. I have asked Archana to come and pick me up. We will be at the office at 6 p.m. After the meeting, she will take me home."

"Ah, okay sir. See you at the office at 6 p.m. Bye for now."

"Bye."

Okay, today I will ask Saran to send a boat to this island to rescue all those people. I really hope he agrees. I will have to think about what I am going to say to him.

* * *

At around 3:30, there was a knock on the door, and when Ravi opened it, Archana walked in.

"Hi Dad, how are you?"

"I am okay my dear. I miss home. I haven't seen your mom in such a long time. How is she doing?"

"Well, she misses you a lot too. She is always worrying about how you are doing. I told her that the hospital is going to discharge you tonight. So, she is really looking forward to seeing you."

"Yes, me too. Listen, dear, the appointment with Mr. Saran has been confirmed for 6 p.m. today. What time do we need to leave to be there by then?"

"Well, given it is going to be rush hour, we'd better leave around 4:30. I will pack your stuff."

Archana and Ravi packed up all my stuff and helped me change into a fresh set of clothes. Around 4 p.m. we vacated the room, and Ravi wheeled me towards Archana's car after we checked out of the hotel.

Once everything was loaded into the car and I also got in, I said to Ravi, "Thank you so much for helping me all these days, Ravi."

"Don't mention it sir, it was my duty. Please take care of your health sir," he said. He turned to Archana and added, "Bye ma'am, I will go now."

"Thank you Ravi," said Archana, "thank you for everything."

Archana got into the car, and we set off to the offices of Saran Airlines in Kalasipalyam.

What am I going to say to Saran? How am I going to convince him to send a boat over to the Maldives? Has what I have done for Saran Airlines in the last few weeks racked up enough in Mr. Saran's mind for him to agree to what I am about to ask?

"There is a lot of traffic today Dad," said Archana, interrupting my thoughts.

I looked out the window. "Ah yes, there is. The roads of Bengaluru have gotten so much busier lately. When I first started working for Saran Airlines, there were nowhere near this many cars and two-wheelers on the road."

"Hmm, but I think we have enough time to make it. By the way, what are we meeting Mr. Saran for today? Haven't you already completed all the work?"

"Well, I want to ask him for something my dear. As compensation for the work I did."

"Why Dad? I did not know you were doing all of this work for money. Besides, we have medical insurance to cover any of your treatment costs. What will you do with this money?"

"I did not do it for the money, but what I did has helped them a lot, so I want to ask for something in return. Maybe the money will be helpful to someone if not me."

We made it to the office at 5:40 p.m., and luckily Archana found a parking spot right in front of the door. Archana got the wheelchair out from the back, unfolded it, and helped me get out of the car and into the chair. She then locked the car and wheeled me into the office.

We went up to the reception and let the person at the desk know that we were there to see Mr. Saran and that we had an appointment at six. The person picked up the phone and spoke briefly before letting us go to Mr. Saran's office.

At the door, Archana stopped the chair and knocked.

"Come in," we heard Mr. Saran's voice say from inside the room.

Archana opened the door and pushed my chair in.

"Come on in," said Mr. Saran. "Niyogi, so nice to see you again. How are you doing?"

"I am doing well Mr. Saran, how are you? I don't know if you remember my daughter Archana."

"Yes of course, I remember. How are you Archana? It has been many years. Please take a seat."

"I am doing well, Mr. Saran; it is very nice to see you too," said Archana, taking a seat next to me to my right.

"I wanted to say how grateful we all are for your father. In spite of your father's health, he has stepped in to take up and successfully complete such a big project for us. Not to mention he helped us trace so much money that we thought we had lost. He is so brilliant that neither retirement nor his illness could stop him from doing what he does best. Even after all these years, he still has so much to teach our accounting staff."

"That is very good to know sir," said Archana, taking my hand in hers.

"So, Niyogi, Kiran showed me the work that you both did and we have already sent that off to our board of directors for review and also to KPMG for them to review the same. I believe that what you did will help us save a lot of consulting costs."

"Very good Mr. Saran."

"So, Niyogi, tell me how I can compensate you for all the work that you did," said Mr. Saran. "Ask me what you want, and I will see what I can do."

"Mr. Saran, I want to ask you for a boat trip. There is an island that I have been wanting to go to for a while, and I want to ask if you can help arrange a trip to that island for me." I could feel Archana's curious gaze boring into me from the side.

Mr. Saran burst out laughing. "Are you serious?" he asked. "Are you sure you don't want me to pay you as remuneration? I will be happy to pay you up to 50% of what I would have had to pay the consultants."

"No Mr. Saran, I have no need for money. I have enough money. What I want is a trip to this island."

"Oh, you are serious," said Mr. Saran, still smiling. "Well, if that is what you want, we can surely arrange it. What island do you want to go to?"

"Archana will tell you."

Archana was caught totally by surprise; she did not seem to know what I was talking about. "What island Dad? What are you talking about?"

Now it was Mr. Saran's turn to look confused. His eyebrows knitted together, and his hand came up to his chin. He was probably wondering if I had gone bonkers. "Do you know what island your dad is referring to Archana?" he asked.

"Uh, I am not entirely sure, Mr. Saran. Dad? Did we speak about an island?"

Obviously, Archana did not understand what island I was referring to. I had given her no heads-up.

"Mr. Saran, I have not been entirely truthful with you," I said. "The reason I offered my help was so I can ask you for this. My daughter has a friend called Gopika. Gopika's son is on an island in the Maldives. What is the name of the island Archana?"

Understanding dawned on Archana's face and she smiled. "Oh...that island is called Khiyalee. It is one of the islands that is farthest from the capital city, Male."

"On that island, Mr. Saran, are around two hundred people who were working in a mine. For some reason, the company that owned the island and the mine was shut down and it went bankrupt. All those people were left on the island, unable to get back home because no one has been able to offer them transportation," I explained.

"And since the whole world was plunged into COVID, no government has come forward to help these people, as all resources have been tied up in fighting the pandemic. What I want to ask in return for the work that I did is that you send a boat to this place to pick up all of these people and bring them to India so that they can find their way home."

"Niyogi, I have a tremendous amount of respect for what you have done for the company in the past few weeks, especially considering how difficult it must have been to work while fighting your illness. But what you are asking for is ridiculous. You have seen our income and expenses for the last few months, so you must know how much it would cost to charter a boat that large for such a trip to the Maldives."

"My estimate is that it will take around ₹20 million."

"Once again Niyogi, you demonstrate your brilliance in financial matters. I think I agree with your estimate. And I don't understand how you can ask me for such a huge thing as compensation for what you have done for us. Not to mention the bureaucratic nightmare that we would have to go through to make this happen. We would have to get permission from both the Indian and the Maldivian governments to make this happen. It is impossible.

"How do you think I can justify such a big expense in the face of all the losses we are incurring due to the same pandemic that affected these people you are talking about?"

I had expected to get rejected by Mr. Saran, but I was not ready for how sad it would make me feel. All the pains that I had taken, all the sneaking around I had done...all of it had come to naught.

"But Mr. Saran, these people are helpless, and I am sure they need immediate assistance with food and medicine. Who will help them if you don't?"

"Niyogi, if you had told me before that you were doing all of the work to ask me this, I would have told you right then that it was impossible. You could have saved yourself all the trouble. You can't spring this on me now and call it compensation for the work that you did. I never asked you to do this work in the first place. In fact, I went out of my way to accommodate you in the hotel and provide you with around-the-clock care. What you are asking for is ridiculous. I am sorry, I cannot help you with this. All I can offer you is ₹1 million as compensation for the work that you did and as recognition for everything you have done for the company in the past."

I had expected Mr. Saran to refuse me. I expected him to think that I was asking for too much. But still I was hoping for more. I was hoping for the slightest chance that he might agree.

"I am sorry for putting you in this position Mr. Saran. I understand your reasons behind not wanting to do what I am asking."

Mr. Saran sighed. "I am truly sorry to disappoint you like this Niyogi, but there is nothing I can do."

"I will take my leave and go home. Thank you for listening to me at least." I turned to Archana. "Let's go home dear, I have done all that I can."

"Okay Dad, let's go," said Archana. She brought her palms together and said to Mr. Saran, "Thank you for hearing my Dad out Mr. Saran, and for giving him a chance."

She then got up, unlocked my wheelchair, and started turning me towards the door. And that was when a new thought came to me. I raised my hand and said, "Mr. Saran, can you give me two more minutes of your time? I will then leave and not bother you. I know of a way this trip can benefit you."

"Go ahead Niyogi," Mr. Saran said.

"I am sure the pandemic has put the thought of travelling out of people's minds. And I know that, as the travel restrictions are slowly lifted, you will see more and more people thinking about travelling again. What better way to bring the name of Saran Airlines to the top of people's minds than with an altruistic gesture like this one? If you offer to rescue those people, I am sure it will get a lot of attention from the press. And when it does, the company's brand recognition will surely soar. That might help Saran Airlines get a lot of bookings when people start travelling again."

"Do you have any financial projections to share to support this idea, Niyogi?"

"I don't, Mr. Saran. This idea came to me just now. But I am sure Kiran will be able to calculate the ROI, and your marketing department can also help think about the viability of what I am proposing."

"Hmm, I don't know about that Niyogi. I don't see much value coming from this."

"I do hope you'll think about it, Mr. Saran, but like I promised, I won't waste your time anymore. Good evening."

Archana wheeled me out to her car and helped me in. Then we left to go home. I was looking forward to seeing Ramani, who I missed terribly.

Chapter 17 - Ramani

From the moment Archana called to tell me that her father was coming home, I couldn't sit quietly. These past two weeks were the absolute worst two weeks that I had endured in a long time. I found it hard to sleep, rest or do anything useful. All I did was worry about how my husband was coping alone in the isolation ward.

I couldn't go and see him or talk to him more than a few times. I was absolutely furious with the whole medical system for locking him away from me. I even asked Archana to take me to the hospital so I could ask the doctors to let me stay in the same ward. I did not care if I got COVID. As long as I was allowed to stay with my husband, I would have been happy, but that did not happen.

I stood on the balcony looking down, waiting to see Archana 's car. At around 8 p.m., I finally saw her car pulling into the parking entrance. I ambled my way to the door and then to the elevator and waited for them to come up. It took way longer than I had hoped for. Just when I was about to press the elevator button to go down myself, the door slid open, and there was Archana standing behind the wheelchair with Vikram, my husband, sitting in it, a bag of clothes and medicine in his lap.

He looked worn out and dejected. He had a sheepish look on his face and dark circles under his eyes.

"Hi Ramani," he said, "I am home."

"Well, it's about time. Give me that bag. Are you hungry?"

"Hmm."

All three of us went inside and I put his bag aside. I would have to wash the clothes later.

"Do you want to take a bath?" I asked.

"Later," he said. "I want to tell you something."

"Archana, can you heat up your father's food? I made a carrot soup, and it just needs to be warmed up."

Archana had moved Vikram's chair next to the chair where I usually sat to watch my TV programs. I went and sat down next to him.

"How are you, Vikram? Did they treat you well at the hospital? I don't know how you managed these two weeks; I had the hardest of times. I kept thinking about you."

"Ramani, I was not at the hospital. I was working."

"What? What do you mean you were working? What work? Where were you?"

"I was in a hotel working on a project for Saran Airlines. I was with Kiran Singh. They booked a hotel room for me and arranged for a full-time nurse to be with me. I went to the conference room during the day to work."

"I don't understand. So, Archana lied to me?" Just then I heard a utensil drop to the floor in the kitchen. "She knew the whole time and she did not tell me? And what work? Why did Saran Airlines need you to work? When did they contact you? How come I never knew about this?"

Vikram remained quiet, as he usually did when I was angry.

"Well, don't just sit there; say something."

"The airline did not ask me; I volunteered to work for them. I wanted to do some work for them so I could ask them for something in return."

"You volunteered? Are you crazy? You can barely go to the bathroom by yourself, and you volunteered to do this work? Without telling me a single thing?"

"That boy kept bothering me and kept on asking me for help."

"What boy and what help? Manoj? Did he ask you for help?"

"No. Not Manoj, the other boy, Archana's friend's son."

"Which friend? Archana, do you know what your father is talking about?" Archana did not answer.

"The boy who is stuck on the island, the mining island. What's-his-name."

"What island? You mean Gopika's son? Isn't he on some island in the Maldives?"

"Yes him, but he speaks to me when I am alone. He keeps bothering me and asks for help."

"Oh Vikram. You did all of this because he was talking to you?"

"Yes, he wanted me to help him. He wanted me to send a boat to the island he is on to pick him up."

"And to help him, you did all of this secretly without telling us?" I turned towards the kitchen to see if Archana was hearing this. She was standing at the door listening, and my eyes met hers. "I am so angry with you Vikram. Couldn't you have involved me in this?"

"I was afraid that you would not let me do it if I had told you earlier. I was afraid that you would not think it was very practical for me to try and help. I had to help the boy. He kept bothering me."

Oh my poor Vikram, you did all of this because you hallucinated a voice talking to you? I am so angry with you. And yet, I know your hallucination was not your fault.

"Of course I would not have let you do this stupid thing. But you did it anyway. I don't know how you managed it, maybe my stupid daughter helped you, but you did what you did. Are you done now? Did you finish your work? Or are you going to sneak out again to do more of this foolish work?"

"No, I am done. I finished the work, and we went to ask Saran to send a boat to the Maldives, but he refused...He said he cannot send a boat."

"I don't know how you thought he would agree to send a boat to pick up two hundred people from another country Vikram, but I am not surprised. But don't feel too bad about it. You wanted to help the boy, and you did your best. You tried your best. I am proud of you for trying."

"But I did not help, Ramani. Saran did not agree to send the boat."

"Well, that was never in your hands Vikram. You did what you could. You should be happy that you tried your best."

"Hmm, yes, I tried. I hope the boy also sees that I tried and stops bothering me. I don't know what to tell him. I am helpless now; I did everything I could."

I took Vikram's hand in mine and held onto it.

"I am hungry Ramani."

"Yes, my dear. Archana, can you please bring the soup dear?"

Archana brought the soup in a bowl along with the syringes for injecting it into Vikram's feeding tube, and she set them down on the coffee table in front of us.

"I want to try drinking it myself," said Vikram.

"Are you sure dear? Did you try drinking when you were at the hotel too?"

"No, but I want to try now."

"Archana, can you bring a glass and a spoon for your father?"

Archana brought a glass, and I poured a little bit of the soup into it. I scooped some soup into the spoon and held it to Vikram's mouth.

He took a tiny sip and swallowed it, his Adam's apple bobbing.

"Wow Vikram, you want to try more?"

Vikram took another sip, a bigger one this time.

"Do you want to try drinking from the glass?" I prodded.

Vikram reached out for the glass and took a sip. Then he took another, and another. Soon he finished the soup in the glass.

"I want more Ramani."

I poured more soup into the glass, and Vikram slowly drank all of that too.

"Oh, Vikram, I am so happy! How long has it been since you were able to drink by yourself? This is such good news. Archana did you see?"

"That is great Dad," said Archana, giving Vikram a kiss on his cheek.

"Oh my God, what else do you want? Do you want to try some coffee? It has been a long time since you tasted coffee; do you want to try?"

"Yes, I do, but first I need to go to the toilet. Can you take me Archana?"

Archana wheeled Vikram's wheelchair into the bedroom and helped him get up and go to the bathroom.

I went to the door of the bathroom after a few minutes. "Is everything okay Archana? You have been in there a while?"

"No, it's okay. Dad's almost done; we'll be out soon."

I heard the toilet flush, and a bit later, Archana opened the door to bring Vikram out. She and I both walked him to the bed, and he sat down.

"Do you want to sit or lie down?" I asked.

"I want to lie down."

"Okay, you lie down, and I will go and get you some coffee."

I went to heat up some coffee for him while Archana sat with him in the room.

"Here you go Vikram; I did not make it too hot, okay?" I said, bringing him the coffee.

With help from Archana, he sat up, took the cup and drank the coffee.

"Ahh, it has been so long since I had good coffee."

Vikram finished his coffee and said, "I will lie down for a while."

Archana helped him lie down, and we left to let him rest for a while. Once we were in the living room, I turned to Archana.

"How could you hide all of this from me Archana? Don't you know how worried I was these two weeks? And now I find out that he was not even in the hospital?"

"I am sorry Mom. Dad asked me not to tell you, and he really wanted to work on this project. I thought with all that is going on, he might feel better if he was distracted with work for a bit."

"Hmm, anyway, I am too excited to be mad right now, we will discuss this later. You are not out of trouble yet. I am just so happy your dad was able to drink something all by himself, not depending on the feeding tube. I wonder if he can try solids tomorrow?"

At that moment, I heard something. It sounded like a whisper. "Is your dad calling us? Vikram...did you call me? Let's go and see."

We walked over to the room. Archana entered before me, and I heard her saying, "Dad? Did you call us? Dad? Daddy? Dad?"

I went into the room and saw Archana calling out to Vikram. His right wrist was twisted a little bit, his face calm and serene. He looked ten years younger, with no sign of pain or discomfort. Archana was shaking him to try and wake him up.

I pulled up a chair that was near the bed and collapsed into it. My Vikram was not responding.

"Vikram, Vikram, VIKRAM! Say something."

I picked his hand up and buried my face in it. Was my Vikram gone? Had he left us forever? I could hear Archana calling people frantically, but she sounded so far away.

After a while, I heard the doorbell ring. Archana ran out to the door and came back with the doctor who lives in our building. He came and checked Vikram's pulse and tried his best to resuscitate him. My Vikram did not respond.

"I am sorry madam; Mr. Niyogi is no more. I can prepare a death certificate for you if you want."

I don't know when the doctor left. I could faintly hear the noises in the room; Archana talking to more people on the phone, her phone beeping with notifications of messages and calls.

After an hour, Archana came to talk to me. She hugged me, and we both cried for I don't know how long.

"I have let everyone know Mom. We have to start making the arrangements."

* * *

The next day, we moved Vikram's body to the ground-floor parking lot. He was wrapped head to toe in a white cloth with only his face showing. People came to see him to pay their last respects. His whole family and extended family came, as did a lot of his friends, his former colleagues, including Kiran, his former Lion's Club mates, our neighbours, my friends, and even people with whom we had lost touch.

The painful day continued with rituals and ceremonies as part of his funeral.

Oh Vikram, I hope you find peace. I hope you find yourself released from your ailing body so you can once again become a part of the universe and forever reside in my heart and in the hearts of those who loved you.

Chapter 18

Saran Airlines Comes to the Rescue of Marooned Miners

The Deccan Herald, April 10, 2022
by Mallika Rangaraju

While the world was celebrating the arrival of the new year, Saran Airlines, a leading private airline company based in Bengaluru, has played a major part in rescuing more than two hundred mine workers from the remote island of Khiyalee about eight hundred kilometers from Male, the capital city of Maldives. The mine workers had been stuck on the island of Khiyalee for six months without hope of rescue as the world reeled from the ravages of COVID-19.

When multiple pleas from the families of the miners remained unaddressed, Saran Airlines, which also operates cruise ships, quietly sent one of their ships to bring the miners from the island back home to India.

The ship started from the port of Mangaluru with a skeleton crew and a few family members of the miners who were to be rescued. The island of

Khiyalee was already equipped with a deep port that could accommodate the ship. Once there, the mine workers was surprised to see the ship's crew and their families, as they had no idea that a rescue was underway.

The crew administered basic first aid to those who needed it and provided them all with ample food and electrolytes. The marooned mine workers had exhausted their provisions about two months earlier and were surviving on the coconuts that were available on the island. The rescue mission was managed and supervised by Mr. Kiran Singh, who represented Saran Airlines.

"With the world undergoing such a debilitating pandemic, we had underutilized resources that we were able to deploy to bring these mine workers back home. We are happy to have been able to play a part in reuniting them with their families," said Mr. Saran, the chairman of Saran Airlines, via a statement that was provided by the company.

This reporter also spoke to Mr. Kiran Singh, who said that the rescue would not have been possible without the contributions of some of the past and current employees of Saran Airlines.

The mining company operating the mine on the island had gone bankrupt due to supply-chain challenges caused by the pandemic. They were left with no resources to take the mine workers back to their countries of origin. This rescue mission from Saran Airlines not only helped the workers of Indian origin find their way home, but also helped many foreign nationals who were brought to India first and were then put on flights to their respective countries.

Mrs. Gopika Chandran got the chance to personally go to the island and help her son Rajamouli and others board the ship. Mrs. Gopika could not contain the joy and gratitude that she felt towards Saran Airlines. "I cannot thank Saran Airlines enough for their generosity in organizing this rescue. When Mr. Kiran Singh called me to inform me that a rescue was underway and that I had the opportunity to be part of it, I thought God himself had heard my pleas and sent Saran Airlines and Mr. Kiran to help me."

Rajamouli and another two hundred mine workers are now recovering in their homes, safe and sound, proving that there is something in the world to cheer for and something positive to write about.

THE END

About the Author

S. N. Rao is an emerging author who grew up in Bengaluru, India. He currently lives in Mississauga, Canada with his wife and two daughters. He has a passion for exploring themes of resilience, positivity, and human connection.

Thank you for reading **Mr. Niyogi's Last Audit**. Your opinion matters to us, and we would love to hear what you think! If you enjoyed the book or have any thoughts to share, please take a moment to leave a review on the platform where you purchased it.

You can connect with me on:

🌐 https://www.authorrao.com

🐦 https://x.com/authorrao

Subscribe to my newsletter:

✉ https://www.authorrao.com/stay-connected

www.ingramcontent.com/pod-product-compliance
Lightning Source LLC
Chambersburg PA
CBHW072302130726
47910CB00012B/2412